A Love Present

'His way with words is masterly . . . [The stories] are all well worth reading and some deserve inclusion in any representative selection of the best of Guaranteed Irish.'

Irish Independent

'John Montague's short stories are satisfyingly well-made and sturdy, like a collection of stripped pine furniture — old, familiar shapes, newly exposed. His prose is simple but solid, with little decoration.'

Sunday Independent

'Awash with seamless brilliance, this succinct collection puts him up there with the O'Faolains and McGaherns. A notable compendium of elegant writing running the gamut of hope, dream and emotional pain, this is prose poetry characterised by apparently effortless riches.'

Modern Woman

'. . . confirms his place in that great tradition of Frank O'Connor and Sean O'Faolain . . . [B]e left in no doubt as to the importance of this voice.'

Magill

JOHN MONTAGUE was born in Brooklyn, New York, and raised in Co. Tyrone. He is an internationally renowned poet and writer whose collections of poetry include *The Rough Field* (1972), *The Dead Kingdom* (1984), *Mount Eagle* (Gallery, 1989), and, most recently, *Collected Poems* (Gallery, 1995). His prose works include *Death of a Chieftain and Other Stories* (reissued by Wolfhound in 1998) and *The Lost Notebook* (Mercier, 1987), which received the first Hughes Award for fiction. In 1998 he received the title Ireland Professor of Poetry. He lives in West Cork and in New York.

A Love Present

& Other Stories

John Montague

WOLFHOUND PRESS

First published in paperback in 1998 by
First published in 1997 by
Wolfhound Press Ltd
68 Mountjoy Square
Dublin 1, Ireland
Tel: (353-1) 874 0354
Fax: (353-1) 872 0207

Versions of these stories have appeared in the following:
'The Letters' in *Born in Brooklyn* (1990) (White Pine, Fredonia, NY); 'Mother
Superiors' in *Fortnight*; 'A Prize Giving' in *The Irish Times*; 'Off the Page' in
Planet in Wales and *Tracks* in Ireland; 'Above Board' in the *Irish Press*; 'The
Parish of the Dead' in *Oberlin Quarterly* (1964); and 'The Three Last Things' in
Shenandoah (1997) in the United States. 'Pilgrim's Pad' is a shorter version of *The
Lost Notebook* (Mercier, Cork, 1987), which *Exile* (Canada) printed.

The Arts Council
An Chomhairle Ealaíon

Wolfhound Press receives financial assistance from the Arts
Council/An Chomhairle Ealaíon, Dublin, Ireland.

British Library Cataloguing in Publication Data
A catalogue record for this book is available from the British Library.

ISBN 0-86327-672-5

10 9 8 7 6 5 4 3 2 1

Cover Design: Slick Fish Design
Typesetting: Wolfhound Press
Printed in the Republic of Ireland by Colour Books, Dublin

Contents

For Elizabeth, of course

Study the world … the movement of a column of ants, the structure of a beehive or a wasp's nest … everywhere there is intent, purpose, sometimes misdirected. And also there is category, and class. And then there is the reproductive drive; only amongst humans is this energy known as love, because it has no seasons…. And only we know that death awaits.

after René de Gourmont

I

The Letters

That special silence of Sundays. All the family have gone to Mass. I listen to their steps fade down the road. There are no lorries on Sunday so sounds are clearer: I can hear the crows in Lynch's plantation, the cows on the hill behind the house lowing to each other occasionally between mouthfuls of grass (there might be one looking the bull), the hens in the backyard, ceaselessly chatting about nothing, except one announcing the arrival of an egg. And my aunts' voices dimming down the hill, every second fainter, as though down a well.

* * *

When Aunt Brigid entered the bedroom, I groaned and turned my face to the wall.

'My stomach is hurting,' I said, and managed a realistic hacking cough. I didn't want to go to Mass; I liked the flowers on the altar, the bright vestments, but it seemed to go on forever. I would read the little bit there was in the Missal, or play with my beads, but there was always time left over, and shifting and staring at other people was supposed to be bad, especially when God was looking. And today was late Mass when Father Cush preached a long sermon till everyone's knuckles were raw with cold. He had been to Rome last Easter and could not stop talking about his visit: 'as many statues as people'.

So I groaned again, my face buried in the bedclothes. Aunt Brigid left the room and came hurrying back with a glass of white, foaming liquid. It tasted nasty but it was all in a good cause, so I drank it down while she watched me anxiously.

'It must have been a cold he caught,' I heard her telling Aunt Freda in the kitchen downstairs afterwards. 'He'd better stay in bed a while till it clears. These cold mornings....'

Freda grunted doubtfully, but she didn't bother to climb the stairs and inspect me herself, as she might have done if it had been a schoolday. I had never dared to stay away from Mass before.

* * *

So at long last I was alone in the still-warm bed, which was far nicer than kneeling stiffly on a wooden bench, or fidgeting as Father Cush droned on. But in a few minutes I would be leaving this warmth in order to creak along the corridor, then down the stairs. Because the real reason for my staying at home lay in a cupboard in the kitchen, a book that my cousin Kevin had left behind. I had watched him reading it while he was holidaying with us; had found it once, lying face upwards on a chair, when he had gone for a walk as far as Clarke's, the Protestant farm up the road. There he would play the mouth organ, running up and down the keyboard with his head cocked sideways while the whole family and their farmhands gaped at such light-hearted skills.

SEXTON BLAKE AND THE PEARL OF INDIA, sang the tall letters on the cover. And underneath, in red, the subtitle screamed: *Our Famous Detective Fights the Devotees of the Goddess Kali — Another Thugee Mystery.* In the accompanying drawing a tall pale man in tropical clothes was being strangled slowly with a cord by a small brown man perched like a monkey on his back. And above them shone a milky pearl, lighting the forehead of a mysterious lady with long dark hair and angry liquid eyes. How lovely she looked and yet how strange and violent the scene beneath her — at which she was smiling like the Virgin Mary. I needed badly to discover what it was all about.

When Kevin left, at the end of his holiday, I hovered around to watch him pack. He wrapped his mouth organ carefully inside his pyjamas but he left the precious book behind.

'Perhaps Johnny would like that,' I heard him say, 'though it might be a bit old for him.'

Aunt Freda looked at the cover dubiously, and turned it over.

'I'll put it away for him,' she said noncommittally; 'he has some comics at the moment.'

And I watched her pack it away at the back of the top left-hand drawer of the cupboard, the one where all the photographs and letters concerning family business were kept. Why was she putting it there, and how could they talk as if I was not present? I was sitting at the big table by the window, drawing with a crayon, and I heard and saw everything.

So, in a way, the book was already mine, or would be, and I was not committing a sin, I told the Infant of Prague on the bedroom table as I got up. And yet here I was tiptoeing like an Indian along the corridor, under the large smiling photograph of Uncle John, who had owned this house but died in America. Houses where people used to live are mysterious, and these empty rooms were peopled only when my cousins came to stay. But a whole family had lived in them, not only my uncle and father, but also my grandfather, whose old Bible, large as a flagstone, was in the smoky dark room over the fireplace. There was also a book about the American Civil War, full of illustrations showing bearded men in slouch hats carrying long rifles, or setting up their tents around a campfire. A famous photographer had taken them, sometimes endangering his life. There were no photographs of my father.

Each one of the stairs had a different squeak as I descended. Under the linoleum were copies of old papers which I had helped Aunt Freda to put down, so that we would have the pleasure of reading them in years to come. The death of President Douglas Hyde was described in one, an All-Ireland Football Final in another. And now I was in the silence of the kitchen, with the great black crook swinging over the fire, carrying its burden of black pots and thick-bellied kettles. They were planning to replace it with a stove but I loved the open fire where I could sit watching the flames as I dressed in the morning.

The cupboard drawer was too high for me to examine

properly, so I took the stool from the fire to enable me to look into it. There were several prayerbooks at the front and a wallet of photographs, most of which I had already seen. They were usually taken in the summer when my cousins were up from the South and we went for a holiday to the seaside at Bundoran. And there was the Sexton Blake mystery, a thin volume, neatly tucked in behind the photographs.

As I pulled it out, I saw that there was a bundle of letters behind; an elastic band held them together. I could see from their length and colour that they were foreign; the first one carried what I recognised as an American stamp, with their President's head — F.D.R. was he called? The handwriting looked familiar; could it be my father's? I had so few letters from him, and yet I was always longing for one of those blue envelopes with the big stamps. They were the only proof I had that I existed in the mind of a man I barely remembered seeing.

Now and again, dreamlike fragments of that American past rose in my memory. Wearing earmuffs against the tingling cold of a New York winter. Placing pennies on the shining trolley tracks. The tenement roofs of Brooklyn where one could play, peering down at the people far below: feeling small, I clung to the chimney stacks. A wooden Indian with head-dress and tomahawk in the door of the movie theatre where we went to see Mickey Mouse. He was scampering across the screen, squealing, while Minnie clattered after him in her big clogs. But there were less pleasant memories as well: the wearing heat of summer with water hydrants spouting in the street; the sound of voices raised in anger. Surely it would be right to have a look at the letters and find out a little more than my stray memories? I rolled back the band and opened the first thin sheet of what was not my father's writing but a large fair hand like I now learnt at Garvaghey School.

You asked me how things are going between 'the couple', I wish you hadn't because I'd rather not think about the whole thing.

You know I don't think much of him and events have borne me out. After she came out with the two boys he pulled up his socks and got a job in a grocery business but lost it because of some carelessness. They have a flat in a very rough neighbourhood and seem to quarrel all the time, since he is at home. He comes over to me looking for help but what can I do? He is my own brother but if I can work and drink, why not him?

I stood trembling on the bare flagstones. It was not an ordinary cold I felt but something new to me, a kind of weakening terror. Was this the way grown-ups thought and spoke about each other? The oleographs of St Francis looked down at me from the wall, a tiny army of robins and sparrows around his sandalled feet. A legend of pure love, Father Cush called him. I took out the next letter in the series, looked at the thin light page.

I gave Jim a job last week and we are all keeping our fingers crossed. You know the old story about the rat in the cheese-shop? Well, the point is that the poor rat set out to eat the lot and got so sick after the first day that he gave up cheese forever.

So I hope that working in a speakeasy will make him see what drink can do to people. I certainly wish it would do the same for me, though since I have to keep things going, I keep my head pretty steady. Strange how these years have been so good for me when bad for most people. I fell on my feet in New York doing what our father disapproved of back home, making poteen, that is.

It's illegal here, too, but the boys on the beat are mostly Irish and they turn a blind eye. They call it 'hooch', and do it differently than back home. We distil it in the bath, which is always full. So we have to go next door to McGarrity's to wash, which the children find funny. They are living near me now on the top floor. I forgot to say that the reason I gave him the job is that she's pregnant again, a get-together after one of their quarrels, I suppose.

The sprawling signature read JOHN and was followed by a lengthy PS.

> *If she weren't so hard on him I think he might hold out better. But they squabble like tinkers, and she is much sharper than him, dainty though she seems. The last time she was banging him around the head with a saucepan — it was a daft scene — shouting: 'You're no good, like the rest of your family.' When she caught sight of me she had the good grace to go red with embarrassment. She told me — privately as she says — that she married the wrong brother. And I must say that when she's angry she looks pretty with her big blue eyes, and her hair astray. But I find women more trouble than they are worth, though not you two, of course, sisters are different.*
>
> *The baby is due next February, I think.*

Like a stunned calf, I fumbled through the little packet, to open the very last one: the date was several years later, 1932.

> *I hope you won the law case about the right-of-way to the bog on the top mountain. Anything to do with the law is always so tricky, though I think I got the details right on the map I drew for you. It was quite uncanny to sit here trying to get the details of bogroads, gates, and the length of bog banks right, over here in Brooklyn. I couldn't help wishing I was up on Knockmany Hill, that cool wind on my face. Shall I never see Tyrone again?*
>
> *I regret to say that I have bad news to report from here. She is sick again and in fact has not been really well since the birth. I must say Jim is marvellous with the baby. To see him crooning to it (he still sings quite well) makes me like him all over again. As its godfather I am concerned about it and wonder what will happen to this new John 'Junior' as they say here.*
>
> *I do my best for them but I have not been feeling myself lately, and there are plans to change the drink laws which would close down my business. I told him that if anything happened to me he should think about sending them all home again.*

Finally I understood, standing there with the letters in my hand. I felt the harshness of that lost Brooklyn world again. My stomach began to heave with small, dry sobs, and I felt cold again, colder than I had ever been. But there wasn't that much time, and things had to be tidied up. Still queasy, but determined, I began to rearrange the letters, one after the other, according to their postmarks, and snapped the rubber band around them before slipping them back, behind the lurid cover of the Sexton Blake, which I now did not care if I ever read.

* * *

Across the creaking house then, past my Uncle John's photograph, past the Infant of Prague, I crept, back to bed. I was still shivering but eventually I fell, or cried myself, asleep.

That special silence of Sundays.

I awoke to footsteps coming back up the broad road. The sound of voices, without hearing words, meaningless as gulls crying over fresh ploughland. Gravel grating underfoot, a key grating in the door. I heard my older aunt's anxious voice in the hallway. 'I hope the boy's all right. Maybe it wasn't wise to leave him alone.'

Mother Superiors

Josie Mellon left the village early in the morning by the first train. The stationmaster was surprised to see her, dressed up to the nines, as he explained later to a large audience in the Dew Drop Inn. She wore a wide-brimmed floppy hat that might have belonged to a film star, an old-fashioned coat with padded shoulders, still crimped from its long wait in some cupboard or drawer, and a pair of platform shoes. In one hand she clutched a heavy snakeskin handbag, in the other her youngest daughter, startled and silent. Neither had ever been in the railway station before.

The journey to the county capital did not take long, the little train waving its plume of black smoke over the rushy fields. Brushing past the ticket barrier, Josie ignored the taxis, but marched her daughter on the inside, down towards the distant, spired centre of the town. Once or twice, people looked curiously at the pair, but, intent as a terrier, she ignored them also.

Josie halted before a pair of wrought-iron gates, carrying an elaborate inscription in blue lettering. A handyman working on a flowerbed looked up but did not move to help her as she lifted, pushed and pulled at the heavy gates. Finally she managed to open one, and she and her daughter set off up the gravelled drive.

It was a long walk for the child, especially as her mother kept tugging her by the hand. But there were bright flowerbeds and bushes to look at before they found themselves at the massive front door, to which, the child thought, everything seemed to lead, like an ogre's castle. There was a brass knocker, higher than her head, and after drawing a deep breath, her mother gave it a sudden, smart bang.

When the huge door opened, a starched figure, all black and

white, or black up to the neck and then white above, looked questioningly down at the two strange waiting figures. But Josie did not falter.

'I want to see your boss,' she said in her sharp, nasal Ulster accent, 'I want the Mother Superior. As soon as you can, please.'

It was the nun's turn to look out of place, flustered almost.

'The Mother Superior,' she repeated, in a puzzled tone. 'Do you —' but began to retreat before Josie's steady gaze and insistent demand.

'Aye, the Mother Superior, I need t'll see her,' said Josie, advancing. The nun backed, between two rows of religious pictures, down the bright corridor.

'I'll try and find Mother,' she flung back, 'but she is usually quite busy. You must wait where you are.'

The child found the size of the hall dazzling, like something out of a fairy tale, an empty ballroom in a palace. Everything was so clean and shining, and the holy pictures looked lovely, with pedestalled statues in the corners, big as in a church. And the black and white tiles looked as if you could slide on them; which she began to try. Her mother stood still, pointed, waiting.

The Mother Superior did not take long, bustling through a glass door, rosary beads rattling at her waist, to confront her unplanned visitor. She also was a smallish woman, face scrubbed clean as a new pin, except for the thin, dark shadow of a moustache. As the child sang, or skipped by herself in the unaccustomed spaces of the hall, the two women stood face-to-face, not speaking. The Mother Superior did not offer her hand, looking uneasily towards the door before she frostily enquired:

'You wished to see me?'

'Right, Sister,' said Josie, 'I do indeed. It's about me poor daughters.'

'About your daughters?' Puzzled, polite.

'Aye, I have five, you know. And I'd like you to take the two eldest.'

'Take them?'

'Aye, take them in here. Everyone speaks about the fine big place you've got and the great job you do. I'd like my two to become young ladies too, not like me.'

'And what do you do, Mrs....'

'Josephine Mellon's the name, but they call me Josie, wee Josie — after me father, Big Joe. I was reared hard. Mammy and Daddy both died when I wasn't much more than a cutty. Da was in the Fusiliers and he had a pension but he drank it. I had no chance at all till the War came.'

The Mother Superior waited, at sea but casting desperately for a sign.

'You were in the War?' she managed, baffled. Who could this strange, scrawny little woman be, with her beady eyes, and old-fashioned finery, her funny clothes that smelt of the mothball?

'Ach no,' said her visitor, impatiently. 'Not officially. We'd be Nationalists, like yourself, I suppose: Da was only an accident, the only job he could find. But the Troops were very good to me. I'd known fellas before but never fellas like yon.'

The nun's face was a mask beneath which incredulity simmered.

'You know how it is, Sister, there's always a lot of lonely fellas in any town. But they have no money, our boys, only hit and run. Not like the Yanks, the doughboys, as they called them. They were wild kind.'

The little girl had temporarily exhausted the pleasures of sliding and then staring at a statue of the Immaculate Conception, blue-veiled on its polished pedestal. She came over and stood meekly near her mother, inspecting the strange, serious-looking lady talking to her, with her stiff, dark clothes and severe look. She touched the swinging Christ figure at the end of the Rosary with the tip of her finger, wonderingly.

'Stop, child. Biddy here's the youngest. I'd like to keep her with me till she grows up a bit. She's great wee company. But I'll send her along too if you treat the others well and give them the chance I never got. There's Teresa, and Bernie, and Maria and Agnes. I always tried to give them holy names, to call them after saints. Considering how they came into this world, it was the nearest to a good start I could give them.'

The Mother Superior's face coloured a little; could this be genuine piety or was she being mocked?

'And what does the father think?' she managed, eventually.

'God look to your wit, Sister. Which father? Two of them died in that dirty old War; poor boys, I often pray for them lying so far away from home, without maybe even a cross over them. And before the Yanks came there was one Englishman but he never wrote to me. I believe he was married. The last is Irish though, one of our own. I know her Daddy well.'

Slowly the Mother Superior mastered herself. All kinds of emotions, from indignation to pity, were running riot through her bloodstream. But how had this apparition, so shabby and out of place, yet so defiant, ever conceived the idea of coming to her, to the convent door?

'And who advised you to come here?'

'Everybody in the town told me, all the corner boys. They said you were great, and would surely understand my case. Go to the convent, they said, that's where they'll be sure to take you in.' She paused. 'I thought they were only having me on, like, but then I asked the Blessed Virgin. After all, she was a mother herself, like me, though she only had the one boy. And God knows, where we live in the Back Lane is not much better nor a stable.'

A bell rang and the Mother Superior looked down at her watch. Her whole face had flushed and her eyes no longer faced those of her visitor.

'I'm afraid I shall have to go now,' she said, ducking her forehead. 'But I'll see you out. Perhaps you'll leave your name and address so that I can look into your case, Mrs....'

'Miss,' said Josie emphatically. 'I never caught one of them. Miss Josephine Mellon: everyone knows me.' Her hand fumbled for the door knob. 'I'm away now, anyway. We'll have to go straight back home. I have to make a bite to eat for the rest of them. You know how it is, at that age, you that have so many of them. Mouths gaping wide as scaldies. Come on, now, Biddy dear. I'll get someone to write to ye and then they can read me back the answer when it comes. Good day to you now, Ma'am. It was very kind of you to talk t'll us.'

The Mother Superior stood watching as the pair dwindled down the avenue. Little Brigid ran over to gaze at a flowerbed once and then looked expectantly over towards her mother, who called the child back just as she was bending down to pluck a blossom. Then they rounded the corner, out of sight, and in the distance was heard the insistent whistle of an approaching train.

A Prize Giving

When the doorbell began to sound frantically around six
o'clock, Mike Byrne knew it must be his niece, Samantha, come
to fetch him. And there she was at the door, sporting a mini-
skirt lurid as her painted eyelids. Beside her was a student, a
Trinity student to judge by his scarf, who was clutching her
hand. They were both drunk, he realised, had spent the afternoon trailing through the new desert of Dublin Central, from
oasis to oasis, the Bailey, Davy Byrne's, the long barn of the
College Mooney outside the side gate. But what were they
going to do with the swaying student? He could hardly bring
him to the Prize Giving at the Convent of the Holy Lamb, the
main event of the evening that he and his niece were due to
attend, she as a past pupil, he as their annual guest speaker,
brought by her at the special request of the nuns.

Giggling, she lurched past him into the darkness of the
hallway.

'This is Daniel,' she said. 'He's a philosophy student and he
seems to want to go to bed with me.'

He received the information with the mixture of interest and
disapproval that seemed appropriate to an uncle greeting a
favourite but wayward niece. She clutched his coat, and as he
leaned forward to support her, he could catch the sweetish
smell of gin and tonic off her breath.

'How are we going to get rid of Dan?' she wailed, and let her
head sag on his chest.

It took him one minute flat — years of broadcasting had
taught him how to act quickly when the warning light glowed.
He hardly remembered what he said but soon he was closing the
door firmly behind young Daniel, or Dan. Then he hustled
Samantha, or Sam, up the stairs, though at the second landing

she nearly toppled back into his arms again. When they reached his rooms at the top of the building he stretched her out on a sofa, then hurried off to prepare a makeshift sandwich to sober her up quickly. She had probably not eaten at lunchtime, a cup of coffee, perhaps, in some greasy spoon, before herself and Dan hurried back to hold hands in a dim, smoky pub corner.

When he came back with it on a tray, she was fast asleep and snoring. Mouth wide open, long, damp hair straggling; it was hardly the picture of the perfect past pupil to present to Mother Superior in an hour or two. There was only one thing left to do. He ran a full basin of cold water and half-helped, half-ran Samantha into the bathroom. Then down with her face right into the full basin, glug, glug, glug.

She rose, spluttering and angry. 'W-w-what,' she gurgled and gargled and gagged as he thrust her relentlessly down again. Finally he let her stand upright and confront herself, flushed and bedraggled, still bleary-eyed, in the big bathroom mirror.

'Jesus!' she cried. 'Is that how I look? The nuns will be horrified.' And she began to wipe off her trails of mascara.

While she tidied herself up he made sandwiches for both of them. Moving around his trim bachelor kitchen he noticed that there were still several fingers of whiskey left in the Jameson bottle. There would hardly be much to drink at a convent do, he reflected — just a preliminary snort of sherry, or some other genteel drink, like ginger wine, and then the easily exhausted pleasure of the water jug on the podium.

Besides, despite all his professional aplomb, he was beginning to feel a little rattled. He looked through the window to where a gantry swung over a new hideous building, a bank probably, dwarfing old Dublin. God knows how chilly some of those convent parlours and presbyteries could be, and Samantha would be immediately noticeable, stinking like a little distillery. And if there was anything that made him ache for a drink, it was moral disapproval, disguised as good behaviour. He had first one drink, and then another, to steady his nerves, as he changed into a sober, well-cut suit, and tie, subdued in colour. By the time he was ready, Samantha was too, with face done and clothing straightened, the little snack she had eaten already absorbing the outer layer of her drunkenness. However, she did still look, if not quite tipsy, tiddly, and after he had called for a taxi he had another quick snort himself, to catch up a little. When the second ring came to the front door, the bottle was empty.

* * *

The new and fashionable Convent of the Holy Lamb was at a polite distance outside Dublin, and the road ran through a pleasant wooded park, designated as a Green Belt. Samantha nodded most of the way, although once she started awake from her daze and fumbled wildly for her handbag. 'Mother of God,' she wailed, 'how will I face Reverend Mother?' and began to dab wildly at her damp face again.

'You'll be grand,' he said flatly, and soon they were swinging through the great iron gates of the convent. A late Georgian manor, whose last owner now lurked in a small flat in Cannes, it had taken on a faintly military air, like a civilian fortress, under its new dispensation. What a strange paradox that the religious had taken over the homes of many of the dilapidated gentry, scrubbing away the scents of sin with their prayers, banishing the flowers of evil with innocence and incense. There was an obscure form of historical justice in the change, Mike Byrne thought as the taxi crunched the gravel before the front door.

As he was paying off the driver, he heard a clumping noise behind him. In clambering out of the taxi, Samantha had tripped and tangled her long coat, and was sprawled on the gravel, displaying a considerable extent of leg. And someone was tackling the forbidding entrance door of the convent, which might gape open at any moment, like a portcullis.

For the second time that evening, he leaped into action. Thrusting a few notes into the driver's hand, he turned to haul Samantha up, and managed to have her nearly upright as two nuns came floating through the door. But he was also dusting her down, with the other hand, so that it looked as if he were embracing her. Or so he feared as he wheeled her smartly around to face the advancing nuns who were dipping and ducking towards them, with welcoming cries, like amorous penguins.

'Agnes, Agnes, my child, how lovely to see you! And you've brought your famous uncle, after all. How nice of you, and how fine and well you're looking....'

They were wafted indoors, in a welter of incomplete greetings. 'You forgot to tell me to hide my mini-skirt with my coat,' Samantha/Agnes hissed as they stumbled along the antiseptic corridors.

'Holy Virgin,' invoked Mike, raising his eyes to heaven — only to be confronted with one! Blue, mild, and smiling, Mary trod the serpent down gently with her slipper as the cortège passed underneath towards, presumably, the convent parlour.

They halted before a large oaken door. Sister Mary and Sister Agathon — or so they had introduced themselves since Samantha was too embarrassed to do more than gulp — led the way in, clucking pleasantly. The room was wide and empty, except for the inevitable holy pictures and a large polished table with a set of accompanying high-backed chairs, guaranteed to stiffen any spine. But there were two ample armchairs beside the empty fireplace, and into them he and Samantha sank, grateful but by now decidedly uneasy. Sister Mary had disappeared again and Sister Agathon was on the floor, kneeling before a side cabinet.

'Do you think they're going to leave us here, high and dry?' he queried, apprehensively, surveying the black rump of Sister Agathon.

'We're going to get some tea, God help us,' whimpered Samantha. 'Tea and bloody digestive biscuits. I told you it was going to be deadly.'

Sister Agathon, emerging backwards from the cabinet, gave a wave of victory, like a bear discovering honey in a tree. She was clutching something, a shining silver salver.

'I knew we had one!' she said, triumphantly. And then: 'But where are the nuts?' She dived into the cupboard again, a foraging squirrel this time, and was still absorbed in her search when the door opened and Sister Mary came back in, smiling.

She had a bottle in either hand, holding them out before her, by the neck, like a wine merchant in an off-licence. But by the shape of the bottles it was whiskey, not wine, and behind her flowed a whole troupe of nuns, large and small, old and young, and all of them beaming. With glinting glasses and laundered cheeks they reminded him of a flotilla of ships, and not old-fashioned sailing ships, but trim coifed yachts, enlivening the sea with contrast and colour and movement:
Sister Aquinas – Sister Maria Dolorosa – Sister Immaculata – Sister Attracta – Sister Francis Borgia – Sister Augustine – Sister Ignatius – Sister Mary Alacoque – Sister Scholastica – Sister Perpetua.

Mike and Samantha shook their proffered hands, smiled back into their delighted faces and then settled back into their leather chairs while the nuns swirled expectantly around. They did not have long to wait, for Sisters Mary and Agathon were busy as barmaids. The salver was now graced with the two open bottles of whiskey and not only one but several packets of nuts and cocktail scraps. Sister Agathon had foraged well: even to someone used to receptions, like himself, it was a fair do. And Sister Mary had a lethal hand with the whiskey, the water just squeaking in at the top of the glass, as an afterthought; Mike found himself sucking in the meniscus. Soon they were all gabbling away happily, lapping the amber liquid.

'You see,' said Sister Agathon, 'we were going to have tea but Mother Superior phoned to say that she was on her way over. It seems she's a great fan of yours, as indeed we all are. So we decided to have a reception afterwards, and warm up with a quiet drink first. I hope you don't mind.'

He glanced over at his niece, Samantha alias Agnes; no, it

was the other way round: he had just got used to her new name for her new self, since she went to college. She was babbling away with a whole group of nuns, so intently that her skirt was riding her ripe thighs. Apart from the nuns' habits they looked like girl friends gossiping in a lounge bar, thick as thieves. What could they be gostering about? She was certainly not explaining to them, as she had to him recently, that she could no longer bear the name Agnes because of its religious implications. He didn't get much time to speculate because his own entourage was going strong, brimming with surprisingly informed questions, and never letting his glass level sink for a minute.

It was about the fifth whiskey, he thought afterwards, when Mother Superior arrived. She was lugging a side of smoked salmon and, between herself and the two younger Sisters riding shotgun with her, the larger part of a crate of wine. He stood up and made a clumsy attempt to bow slowly, but she brushed away his formality by raising the glass of whiskey she had been given as she put down her offerings.

'To a splendid prize giving,' she said, and clinked her glass against his. 'It was so nice of you to come. And little Agnes' — she turned her formidable but friendly glance on his niece — 'My, she has grown. She is no longer our little lamb; that was her nickname here, you know, *agneau*, a little lamb of God, she spent so much time in the chapel. I'm sure that's changed; did she ever tell you she once thought of joining us?'

Mike Byrne nearly choked on his whiskey; this was the first time he had ever heard of a lamb being let out of the bag! He was going to deny all knowledge when he caught the imploring eyes of his niece and nodded instead. 'Of course,' he muttered, and accepted the fresh whiskey that flooded into his glass. Several more drinks down, he began to panic. The conversation was fascinating but was he ever going to meet the convent girls, the ostensible object of his visit?

Finally Mother Superior seemed to give an invisible signal and they trooped out in a long procession towards the study hall. And just as he was beginning to worry about the embarrassing side-effects of such a torrent of drink, Sisters Mary and Agathon appeared at his side, like two bodyguards.

'You might need to pay a little visit here, first. Father Flynn always goes in before Mass.'

Here was a discreet toilet up a side passage, probably close to the chapel. Everything was bright and clean, and he was unburdening himself with relief when he remembered that the two nuns were only a few feet away in the corridor, within earshot of his waterworks. His flood had been splashing so merrily that it sounded more like a horse than a human. He tried to modulate the volume but he was still tipsy enough to forget where he was and emerge, adjusting his fly, as though he were in some grotty pub. But if the nuns saw or heard anything they gave no sign but shepherded him towards his destination, still chatting warmly.

Propped up high on a dais at the end of the hall, with the décor of the school play behind him, and flanked by smiling nuns, he discharged his prize-giving duties with automatic professional skill. Mother Superior began with a short eulogy of his works and pomps, describing him as a social catalyst, one of the first to try to compel the Irish to take a hard look at themselves. Was he a Catholic catalyst, he wondered facetiously, or a Protestant catalyst? But he did manage to weave a few pointed references to modern problems, like birth control, and contraception, into his general encomium of youth. Things had changed in Ireland, he said, but between liberty and licence there was a delicate balance, which their training here would help them to discern. There would be difficulties, because Ireland was still an island of belief set in a sea of secularism, but things had relaxed, and freedom was far better than old-fashioned frustration. What else could he say, looking out on a wave of young faces, eager, laughing, and sometimes surprisingly pretty? But pace themselves, he suggested: life was a marvellous gift but to enjoy it properly one must show one's gratitude.

Altogether pretty painless, he felt; the sound of polite clapping filled the hall, as each successful candidate came tripping up for her prize. The only times he felt uneasy were when a particularly fulsome remark seemed to get confused with a hiccup, and afterwards when, trying to adjust his seat, it nearly disappeared off the platform. He clutched for the table to right himself, and it also began to teeter. Luckily no one seemed to notice, and as he stepped carefully down, Mother Superior took his arm contentedly.

'Well done,' she said. 'You gave them something to think about. And now we can relax.'

And what had they been doing before, he wondered, as with a firm hand Mother Superior piloted him away, to the renewed sound of clapping. He had never seen so many young girls in his life, dividing like the Red Sea before him. And they were all smiling, perfectly at ease in their setting. Where was the grim Ireland of his youth; indeed, where were the chilly nuns of yesteryear? Even Samantha seemed to be out of touch, so the change must have happened recently, or she had succumbed to the usual anti-clerical cliché, and remembered only the bad about her boarding-school days.

He was happily planning a programme on the Modern Nun when he was ushered back into the convent parlour again. Somebody had been at work, for it was transformed — as well as the smoked salmon, now tastefully sliced and displayed, there was a fine large bird, a roast tom turkey with its cooked legs cocked in the air. The wine bottles were lined up ready for battle, red on the right, white on the left, with what was left of the whiskey in the front. Had they really drunk that much? There were only a few glasses left in each bottle, and by the same token it seemed as if the wine would soon suffer a similar fate as it was splashed into thin-stemmed glasses.

Plate on his knees, glass in hand, he found himself rattling away with Mother Superior as if they had always known each other. The most impressive thing was that the conversation was not restricted in any way; she had spent a long term in the mother house in Paris, and spoke of things, Irish and otherwise, with the frank interest of a cosmopolitan, or at least someone who had lived in the wide world. She did speak of declining vocations but also of Women's Liberation; what did he think of it?

Before he could gather his thoughts, she gave him her own strong opinion — she found it had been too long delayed and consequently a shade strident. But there still were areas left untouched — priests, for instance, were never mentioned. And yet they were the ultimate citadel of Irish male chauvinism, masculine dodos who expected nuns to lay a boiled egg every time they appeared, in their lone majesty. Father Flynn always brought his underwear with him when he came to say Mass, as if the convent were a laundry. And he hung around afterwards, wolfing down a big fry.

And many Irish women had mistakenly given this kind of treatment to their sons, ignorant gulpins who sat at the top of the table, waiting to be served. This priestly syndrome had spoiled many Irish men forever, waiting for women to dance attendance on them. Not only could they not handle a washing machine, they could hardly boil a kettle. And if they were so inert about such everyday details, so deliberately helpless, what must they be like in bed? She knew it was not a nun's place to speculate, but she thought the pleasure quotient must not be high. To think of her little charges (all of whom now received instruction in anatomy) in their clumsy, ignorant hands, made her blood boil.

Mike Byrne lay back, roaring with laughter. This handsome, civilised, humorous woman was a terror when she got going; he loved her ferocity. It was the best sport he had had in a long time; instead of tea and biscuits in a chilly parlour, here he was pleasantly fluthered and blessed amongst women. What further surprise did the evening hold?

It came soon enough. The oaken door opened and a last nun came sailing in, an old nun, as old as the hills. And she sailed straight towards him, with, to his astonishment, open arms. 'Mikko,' she said, using the childhood diminutive, 'I bet you don't remember me from Adam.'

Mike Byrne rose hesitantly from the depths of his armchair. Clearly the scene had been set for some kind of exchange, for all the other nuns went silent, waiting with interest to see what happened. Either the old girl was dotty — but how could she have known his nickname? — or she had been bragging of knowing him at some time in the past. But when and where? He knew his hair was already grey and there was a middle-aged paunch growing, despite the Canadian exercises, but she must be fifteen or twenty years older than him. All his professional muscles began to flex, reluctantly forcing themselves through a cloud of alcohol; it was part of his job never to forget a face. Abundant grey hair, with some flecks of red, a broad, still freckled face, a familiar accent; not nasal Dublin, not a Western lilt, but vowels flattened by a pleasant drawl. Ah, yes....

In his memory's eye he saw a farmhouse in the Irish midlands, beside a broad lake. He went there every year for his summer holidays and he and his cousins could borrow a boat to go fishing or swimming. It was a lonely spot, but in some way charmed; the swans would come drifting in to beg for bread beside the little jetty where boats rode. He had sat there late in the evening, listening to a stocky young woman, the eldest daughter of the house, as she told him of her plans for the future, her secret wish to become a nun. Even if she had wanted it, marriage was out of the question; there was hardly a man left in the area: except for a few heavy farmers, they had all emigrated. The little village was closing down; the anvil of the blacksmith would never ring again, after he left down his hammer. In all the emptiness, this accelerating change, she saw only one constant: the love of God. She had decided to dedicate herself to Him, and the small boy was very impressed as she told him shyly of her wish. She had come home obediently from the convent, when her mother died, to help look after the younger children, but when they were fully fledged she would go to speak to her father again....

'Mary Reilly!' he said — and they collapsed into each other's arms — after forty years. Whatever test, or contest, was involved, they had both passed it, for when he turned, all the nuns were up and smiling. The evening had come to its natural end, or climax, as, with an odd combination of personal warmth and ritual politeness, the nuns came up to embrace him. Mother Superior was first, of course, saluting him warmly on both cheeks, à la française. Sisterly hug or polite peck, they all had their say, after which he and Agnes were shepherded to a waiting car. His last image was of them crowded on the steps before that same great door, waving their arms like wings.

On the way home, the headlights of the taxi illuminating the startling green of the early summer leaves, he lay back in his seat, wondering. If he ever tried to tell the story of this evening, who would believe him? Indeed did he believe it himself? A whole evening spent getting riotously drunk with nuns, ending up with his being kissed by an entire convent? Content and sleepy, he decided that maybe it had never happened, that it was all some kind of waking dream. He looked over at his niece; she had fallen asleep, or passed out again, a smile of total contentment on her young face. Dream or not , she clearly did not wish to wake from it, and he could hardly blame her, for neither did he.

Off the Page

A lecture engagement brought Seán up from Dublin on the train, a bit dismayed to find that it was no longer the smooth Enterprise Express he remembered, which linked the two capital cities of the two parts of Ireland twice a day. The train had a kind of tattered wartime look and there was a bomb scare beyond Dundalk, near the Border.

After the train had been searched, he wandered towards the dining car. Waiting for someone to come to take his order, he pondered over the paradox that there seemed to be two menus, one the familiar overpriced one of CIE, the other announcing an Ulster Fry. That stirred a pleasant memory from his graduate student days in the North — fat slices of fried potato cake flanking back rashers — but he found out when the attendant came that he could have that only on the way down, not up, when CIE were in charge. Seán gave in with bad grace, especially as the alternative menu card had not been cleared away, thus arousing false hopes of getting into the old atmosphere. And in any case he was not sure that the attendant was right; in his experience, most minor officials managed to get everything arseways, or baw-wise, to use a Northernism. But by now the train was pulling through the Gap of the North, and the South Armagh Hills always stirred him: there was something timeless about them, a stony patience that made factionalism seem absurd. But what was that hovering near the summit, above the Hag's Lake, dipping and rising? He recognised with distaste the flickering hornet shape of an Army helicopter.

Seán had to run the gauntlet of the bar on the way back; it had opened again, just after the Border. He was surprised but pleased to be hailed, not once, but twice. A stray Englishman who had heard him lecture at Cambridge on the Eighteenth

Century; an in-law he had not seen for years. It was an unusual haul and Seán thoroughly enjoyed himself, with the Black Bush flowing; the Englishman doted on Ireland, and the Southern relative was planning to buy a house in Belfast, since both his daughters were studying there. So a pleasant wrangle ensued, spoiled only when another attendant refused to accept the Englishman's Irish money, now that they were across the Border. They settled it among themselves, with grace and good humour, and a good few rounds later, they were entering the outskirts of Belfast.

They shared a taxi to the centre of the city but there Seán's good humour soon soured. How had he become so out of touch that he had not realised that there was a new station, replacing the gaunt but familiar shape of Victoria Street? Thank God the Ulster Bus Depot was still there at least; he would be able to get rid of his baggage. But the Baggage Department was closed and he stood baffled in the middle of the hall, with one hand growing longer than the other, his overnight bag and briefcase feeling as if they were loaded with stones. He had been looking forward to a few hours on his own in Belfast before he joined his colleagues at the university; that was why he had chosen the earlier train, but the possibilities for pleasant reminiscence seemed to be evaporating fast.

The little hotel opposite the station, for instance, where he had often stayed on his way through; the rooms were makeshift but the night porter was most accommodating: it had been a favourite after-hours watering hole for all sides, but now it was gone, gone completely, a waste ground. He had stayed in the Crown too once, a feat since its rooms were as dilapidated as its front was magnificent. He had a consoling conversation with one of the barmen there about old times. No, they no longer sold Single X, the old flat porter with the cheesy taste, but the pint was good, slowly pulled with its clerical collar of creamy froth. And the chat around him was much the same: Belfast working class intent on the Sports Page ('I don't think the fukken dog will fukken win' or 'The odds are too fukken high', the same familiar adjective applied to greyhounds, boxing, soccer as if they were all the fukken same). Two or three still wore dunchers, flat working-class cloth caps.

There was a sprinkling of middle-class types and the Bar Menu seemed to have become a shade classy: wine could be bought by the glass, hardly a beverage favoured by either Shankill or Falls. And did the windows not look a little different? The barman told him that some had had to be replaced, after a bomb blast; a reprisal, he said, looking around carefully, but not by the side you'd expect. The jacks was unchanged, though, and he watered the intricate art nouveau patterns of the rose porcelain with pleasure, after his first pint. When the barman brought him his second drink to one of the wooden booths, opulent in its carving as a medieval confessional, with griffins and other strange, fantastic animals interlaced, he explained his problem with his luggage.

'Ah, sure you can leave them with me, behind the bar. By the looks of you, there's nothing more dangerous than a few books in them. But don't take too long: I go off duty at six, for me tea, and the next man mightn't know what the hell they were.'

And so Seán got his walk through central Belfast, at last. He had never really liked the city in the way he loved the melancholy of Georgian Dublin; it was, after all, a typical mid-nineteenth-century British industrial city, which had largely lost its link with the country around it, now often suburban, like Bangor and Lisburn. But he had grown used to it during his year as a graduate student, spending afternoons sitting at a desk in the Linen Hall Library, raising his head from some rare book to stare at the pseudo-classical weight of the City Hall. Both were still there and he wandered up Royal Avenue, a bit disconcerted to find the Bank Buildings open, but Robinson and Cleaver closed. This sudden shuddering gear-change of emotions was disturbing: people were indeed shopping in the city centre but they had to pass through checkpoints manned by

black-clad officials. Hadn't there been a bookshop there, or had
he only dreamt it? And a hotel — he felt disorientated, only
half knowing where he was; the only thriving industry seemed to
be security systems, advertised on every second door and window. Chubb Alarms, Shorrock, Modern Alarms, Guard Dogs,
Control Zone — it was a new bleak form of semiotics that
flustered him. There were two sets of taxis, both black, but he
didn't know which queue to join, so he decided to hoof it to the
university, picking up his gear along the way.

* * *

The lecture went well, Seán thought. As usual, it took him a
while to warm up himself and his audience, to slide back into
the Eighteenth Century until it was no longer history but the
real choices of real people, some of whom had lived in their
home area, like Thomas Russell, arrested in his own Linen Hall
Library. To illustrate a point about historical change, he
mentioned his walk through Belfast, how it had moved and
saddened him to see so many of the landmarks he had known as
a student obliterated. What would the United Irishmen think of
the New Ireland, North and South? It was not the vision they
had campaigned and sometimes died for; he hoped that a small
flame of tolerance and intelligence still flickered in some hearts.
One of the ironies of the present bombing campaign was that it
meant that people were destroying their own childhood
memories. He sensed a slight unease in his audience at this
divagation, so he moved back to his analysis of the ideas of the
Enlightenment, the way they had influenced America as well as
France. As he came to a graceful halt, gathering his papers,
there was a steady ripple of applause. History was great stuff to
discuss, when it was at a safe distance. The chairman said a few
words and then they surged quietly to the bar, across the street
in a private club.

He was halfway through his first drink when he felt a tap on
his shoulder. It was so light that he ignored it at first until it

became more insistent. Turning, he saw a face he recognised, the once-familiar face of someone he had been at school with, but now sharpened, shadowed by age. A determined, almost hard face, and not smiling.

'Why, hello, Danny Cowan,' he said. 'Nice to see you again.'

Danny nodded, but he did not seem interested in the courtesies or in the people who were swirling around — teachers, officials, a handful of students.

'I want to talk to *you*.' The 'you' was emphasised.

'But you are talking to me,' laughed Seán.

The other made a dismissive gesture. 'Not with shites like these around.'

Seán went silent, surprised. 'What about tomorrow, then?' he said at last. 'You can call for me at the staff club, surely?'

'Now. I need to speak to you now.'

Seán looked around at the crowd. They seemed happy enough, and he had spoken to the few graduate students. Still, it would be impolite to desert his hosts. 'How long will it take?'

'Not long. Only a brief minute.' Or had he heard 'briefing'?

'Will you drop me back before this place closes?'

'Aye.'

He excused himself to the chairman of the meeting and a few other staff members. They looked curiously at Danny but when he said 'schoolfriend', they nodded. 'We'll hold the fort for you here. Get back before the well runs dry, though.'

On the drive through a darkened Belfast Seán sought for some common subject of conversation. But his companion was laconic, brusque to the point of unpleasantness. Danny had married a good-looking girl, he remembered, also militant when she was at the university. They had both been involved in protests, some of them leading to jail terms. But he had not been heard of in recent years, since the bombing campaign began.

They were stopped at two roadblocks, but Danny handled the soldiers with almost contemptuous ease as they poked their heads into the car. Once, as a Gloucester was leaning his rifle on the slope to probe in the back of the car, Danny pushed the weapon aside and held the few objects up for inspection: a rag doll and a box of pamphlets.

'Did no one teach you how to handle a rifle properly? It is not a broom handle you're holding, you fool. And you might take one of those away with you to read instead of your gutter press: you might learn why you are over here.'

The soldier started, but seemed to accept the rebuke. Afterwards, Seán realised why — he was responding to a tone of voice, the crispness of someone of the officer class addressing a common soldier.

'That was a good trick,' he said admiringly as they moved again through the darkness. But his companion did not seem to understand, or even care, what he meant. Sandy Row, Grosvenor Road, the Royal Hospital, barbed wire, bombed or blackened buildings, the grim décor of a wartime town seemed to go with his silence. There was only an occasional shaft of light with pub windows glinting through heavy shutters. Now it was a poorer district, with identical redbrick houses, little hutches where the Catholic working class bred, survived, clawing out a living. Even in the night-time there was a sense of desperation, cramped lives behind neat curtains; a few yards away a wall was raised to cut off this area from a similar Protestant one — a building-block version of the Berlin Wall, a sectarian Lilliput.

But the house they finally stopped before, much further on, was quite respectable, a semi-detached with a garage, and a pocket-handkerchief lawn. 'Edenview' it was called, he saw in the car's headlights, but when he made an appropriate laughing comment there was no response; any attempt to lighten the proceedings was, it seemed, out of place. At the door his tall wife (Eve?) appeared, and he found her as pleasant-looking as he had remembered but, like her husband, much more tense, harsh almost. Was this the inevitable erosion of feeling caused by living in such an atmosphere?

After a few ritual greetings, she disappeared into the kitchen, and he was left alone with Danny. Seán looked expectantly around but there was no drinks cupboard. They sat opposite each other in identical armchairs — part of a wedding suite? — for several minutes, but nothing was said. There were a few wedding pictures, a library which seemed to be largely political, and a copy of the 1916 Proclamation over the fireplace. Then the tea trolley was wheeled in, china tea cups and a jug of the same design, an already segmented sponge cake and biscuits. As his wife dispensed the little cups of tea, Danny cleared his throat:

'You should never say that.'

Seán left it for a while, balancing his tea carefully, before he answered. 'What?' he said, then, 'I gave an hour's lecture.'

The silence was flinty. He tried again, with teasing humour this time. 'Come on, Danny, I didn't know you were a student of the Enlightenment.' Again, silence, until Danny's wife edged forwards on her chair. 'Was the lecture on lighting?' Both men sniggered, in an embarrassed way. Then, just as Seán began to fear that he was stuck forever in this ice-pack of parlour politeness, Danny leaned forward again, shifting his hams. Whatever about the hungry streets they had passed through, neither Danny nor his wife looked starved — maybe protest could also be a paying proposition.

'You know well what I mean. The remark about Belfast.'

'What remark?' was Seán's first reaction but, as he ran the tape of his lecture back swiftly through his head, he thought he remembered some chance remark, a throwaway comment before he warmed up, or a way of filling in a silence when the current of attention flickered.

'About it being destroyed.'

'But it is being destroyed. And rebuilt. And presumably will be destroyed again. Modern terrorism is a bit like the medieval plague — it comes back.'

'That's not the point, smart alec.'

'Then what is the point? Urban violence has a self-perpetuating quality.'

Despite himself, Seán had begun to feel that not only was he under cross-examination, but that he was, in some sense, to blame for the situation. Otherwise, why should he be trying to justify himself? 'What point?' he repeated again, sharply. 'Come clean, brother,' mockingly. Cowan leaned forward again, and launched into a speech, almost a tirade. At first, Seán wanted to protest, to respond, to discuss, but the man's tone, his chill and relentless intensity, precluded it. His message was simple enough: consciously or not, Seán had said something from a public platform that should not be said and he should never say it again, in his puff.

'You said you felt sorry to see the city so torn and destroyed. That you had known it as a student and that despite its lack of obvious beauty, it meant something to you. Let me tell you that no one, but no one, in this part of the city cares a flying fuck if the whole place was bombed, broken, blasted to hell. You saw those small streets we came through: all that City Hall represents to them is repression, endless repression, dole queues and undying bigotry. So people died for the Crown; more than half of them were from these small streets: they didn't have a choice. Look at the names of the places they live in, old Empire battles, Balaclava Street, Bombay Street, Crimea Street. So for some simpleton like yourself to suggest that this hellhole ever had any good reason to exist is sentimental shite and you know it. You and your history — it's phoney liberals like you fuck things up: you're so unaware that you don't even know that the first sectarian campaign was organised by the British, using the UFF, four hundred dead and tortured. Then when they had started the old hatred machine again, the sappers sealed the sides off, with that wall you saw. You and your history — you can't see it when it hits you between the two eyes.'

The diatribe was impressive, but Seán was not content to let it pour over him — somewhere, he felt, there was a right response. 'But surely memory. Feelings. Emotional deposits over the years. Family.'

'Fuck memory. You sound like Edmund Burke flashing his sword for Marie Antoinette against the French Revolution. All the memories anyone from our side has of this city is dirt, darkness and pain. If a bomb wiped out Royal Avenue and stopped the Albert Clock, I'd howl with joy, not weep crocodile tears about old times. John Betjeman's Victorian City is the nearest thing to a gulag the West has to offer, from the prison ships in Belfast Lough to Castlereagh. So shut your educated mouth when it comes to serious subjects: closet philosophers the lot of you — toilet, more like!'

Seán remained silent. He was used to academic malice but this was on a more desperate level. He remembered a moon-faced colleague, a mother's pet if ever there was one, who seemed to thrive on spite. Someone's book linking the Viking Period and violence in modern Ireland was mentioned and his only comment was 'putrid'. Asked playfully to develop this theme, he had only responded obstinately: 'I mean putrid. Old shite with hairs on it.' Seán had shuddered at the vindictiveness, wondered also at his own naïveté. If the intolerable situation dragged on, they would all become mutants; certainly that one was on the way: the combination of peculiar looks and Ulster's plight already made him look malign as a gargoyle. And now the anal fixation again, a reversion to the war cries of the nursery floor. He couldn't even be sure that Cowan was really angry — he had never once raised his voice, just stared steadily at him with something like indifferent scorn. He ended as he began: menacingly.

'So never say that again from a public platform in this city, *in your life.*'

This time Seán understood what he meant. He rose to leave. 'You'll drop me back, as you promised?'

Cowan nodded and his wife went off to put on her coat. They all three drove in silence back through the now nearly lightless city and Seán did not ask them into the club bar. There the hardy annuals were in session, and Seán was greeted warmly on all sides, with no 'what kept you?' The bartender, an ex-service man who had fought in the desert, and claimed to have driven Monty, pushed a double Bush towards him, with a wink, the drinker's conspiracy against seriousness. 'On the house, Doctor,' he said. 'You're the excuse for this badness.'

Seán laughed relievedly. It was good to be back among friends, he thought, but then had he not been with a friend? His head hurt a little and he felt squeamish as he looked around at the comfortable surroundings, the affable sound of voices raised in friendly dispute or banter, the sudden normality; there didn't seem to be a shitehawk in sight, eager to play the game of Gut the Visitor. But then the Cowans had looked normal, super normal, so the cosiness of this ultimate watering hole might be another mirage. As the full effect of what he had heard that evening came back to him, he excused himself, and hurried to the gents.

The naked neon over the washbasins seemed unusually harsh, garish: he felt as if he had just been on an all-night flight and had been abruptly woken. It glittered like a spotlight off the tiled floor, making him feel sick, or worse: maybe at this very moment some poor bastard was being interrogated somewhere else in the city. But before he could even work out what was wrong with him he found himself looking at his own strained face in the mirror. How could he guess how he would look if he lived in this taut climate? Much of what Cowan had said rang true, though such weasel venom was beyond him. All tenderness, all gentleness was ruled out, all cosy exchange. Yet there was something admirable in this flinty obduracy, like the determination of cave people. Perhaps he needed to be shaken out of his academic reflexes, his incipient pomposity? So history had come off the page and he did not know what to say or do about it; there was no way he could explain what had happened to his waiting hosts, or anyone else. Bracing his hands on either side of the washbasin, he leaned his head over and began to retch. Half-digested biscuits, sponge cake and brown tea spilled out of his mouth in a dirty stream. He wiped his face clean and headed back towards the warmth of the bar, and that full glass.

II

A Love Present

Snobbery begins early. With my neat ankle socks over polished shoes, I was clearly intended to be a cut above the other boys in Garvaghey School, the sons of small farmers and farm labourers. After Easter, as the days grew longer, they came to school in their bare feet. In a few weeks their soles were as tough as the shoe leather they were saving, while I still unpeeled in the evenings sticky socks from soft, white feet.

My aunts wanted it that way: I bore my grandfather's name, and if the family fortunes had dwindled, some day everything might be restored to some mythical position which I couldn't yet understand. But how could they know that I wanted desperately to be like the others, to go slapping my bare feet down the Broad Road, and, joy of joys, to stick my toes in the tar which burst in small, black bubbles as the summer heat came? You cleansed it off with butter, mushy yellow on black, a glorious mixture, thick as axle grease.

And to run through the fields, like a hunter in an adventure story, without bruising a leaf, breaking a twig. Like Leatherstocking, or Fenimore Cooper's poor relation Altsheler, who wrote about the Mexican–American war, planting an early obsession. And above all, Tarzan, Lord Greystoke with his Lady Jane, and pet Cheetah. What they all had in common was the call of the wild. Instead of town suits and ankle socks, I wanted to be clad in animal skins and leap from branch to branch in the forest. Clarke's Wood was a poor substitute for the steaming jungle but imagination could do a lot and I wonder what my aunts would have thought if confronted with me, stark naked, as I balanced in a tree above the river. I leaped from branch to branch, excited by the smell of leaves and peeling bark, the wind on my bare flesh, before dropping into the mud below. Then there was the chill of the stream to cool my excited flesh.

For I was not encouraged to play with the local boys, sup-
posedly because they were too rough. I met them secretly,
though, admiring Gussie's ferret which climbed obediently up
his arm, till it looked like a lady's long glove, of the kind I still
found in our house, remnants of 'auld decency'. But the shriek
of a rabbit seized by its needle teeth was not refined. Outside a
wilder life prevailed, setting gold loops of snares for rabbits,
guddling trout by hand in rocky pools (I only gave up when
bitten on the thumb by an eel), robbing orchards for green
apples and gooseberries, stoning magpies. There the competi-
tion was to be as mustang wild as possible, not good as gold.
How sweet the little speckled trout tasted, roasted over a wood
fire — firm-fleshed, fragrant, the taste of the forbidden.

And the rough games they played! If you didn't watch out,
you would get pushed in the river, or the nettles, or the oozing
dunghill, a perfume hard to explain at home. Summer we
roamed the hills, as far as Knockmany, or climbed into the
mouldering mystery of a deserted house. We had a den among
the hazels where we accumulated stolen goods: sweets I brought
to curry favour, our first cigarettes, pictures of naked women
from *Lilliput*. Rainy Sundays in winter, we sheltered in a barn,
swapping dirty stories. Bulling a cow was a favourite game, large
boy mounting smaller with a squeal of triumph. I did not join in
but watched avidly; perhaps I hoped that I might be pulled in
one day but they left me alone, as if, indeed, I was not quite one
of them. Only when my father sent me a set of boxing gloves
was I conscripted as an equal, though their styles were so ferocious that I was usually content to be referee. I can still see Gus
charging in, a human juggernaut, oblivious to my deft flicks if he
could only land one thunderbolt.

Boxing, leaping the river, playing ball in the Holm; I could
present these as acceptable activities but I kept quiet about our
other secret games, which so fascinated and repelled me. The
only children I was officially allowed to play with were the

Kellys down the road, who owned the new shop, which had largely replaced ours. They had a garden bordering the road, like us, and among the sweet peas and pansies I played with Mary, the eldest, and her puffy-faced brothers, all younger than me. Mary was demure and slender, with swinging pigtails, and perhaps because we were so often thrown together, I began to feel that I was in love with her, a pure devoted love like that inspired by a princess in one of the fairy stories we read together.

She had fair hair, a small mouth that pouted slightly, and light blue eyes, like the most innocent of dolls, or an angel bending its wings in the corner of the chapel. Was my love for her really that pure? Whatever I felt for her, she did not respond. I had to arrange games of hide-and-seek with her putty-faced younger brothers, so that I might find her, cowering in a corner of the garden, and throw my arms around her, crying 'Caught', as I inhaled the fresh smell of her skin, like wet, cut flowers. Or wrestle with the eldest, until he called for his sister's help, and we tumbled together on the lawn under the climbing sweet peas. Once I managed to kiss her, but she must have thought nothing of it, for she stood up and brushed her skirt as if nothing special had happened. There was nothing about her that I did not like; I was especially entranced by the twin trails of slime that so often descended from her slight nostrils. Unabashed, she poked out a tiny pink tongue and licked the snail tracks clean. Such is the power of love that I was fascinated by the sight of that silver syrup, sliding down towards those lips I coveted so much.

'Now, be good, children.' I hear the cry, and see myself and the little Kellys, listening to Uncle Mac on the BBC, from five to six in the evenings. The better-class children of Garvaghey, innocent as Ovaltine and arrowroot biscuits, while that unruly world roamed outside, full of the disgusting games I loathed and partly longed for. The next morning both worlds would meet on the school benches, hardly acknowledging each other.

White ankle socks and swinging pigtails were small defence in the seething turmoil of a country school, with its rituals of defilement.

A favourite sport was spying on the girls' lavatory. The crudest way of doing this was peering through an open seat on the boys' side; there would be a rush to the look-up point, so to speak, when some poor girl went innocently in to pee, and the round, white moon of her leaking bottom was gloatingly described by the boy lucky enough to get his head down first. Because her house was so close Mary never went to the school bog, and I tried not to, embarrassed by the smells, the sniggering prurience. But once Gus got me to climb on the wall that separated the two sections, where we were spotted by the senior mistress, a famous bee. She walloped my companion's thick skull with a giant blackboard ruler but let me off with a pointed reproof about letting down my family's good name.

'There's no excuse for you: you should know better than to behave like an animal.' There was a note of spite in her voice; she had once stayed in our house, and quarrelled with my younger aunt over something. I was thoroughly confused, by now, because Gus and I had become altar boys, patiently instructed by the priest with chalk diagrams on the school floor. The sweet, sickly smell of altar wine, the chink of the cruets, the locking and unlocking of the tabernacle, all that glorious ritual gave another, mysterious dimension to our lives. Should I confide to the priest in the confessional about our secret games, or would he find me unworthy to kneel on the cold marble of the altar? Gus had taken a swig of the altar wine and said it was great, but warned me against saying a word about our shenanigans to Father Cush.

'What we're doing is only natural. Don't you bring the cow to the bull, and haven't you watched the rooster light on the hens?'

Even grown-ups didn't seem exempt from the contradictory pangs of love. Our senior mistress was courting heavily with her future husband; 'lying in all the ditches of the country,' said my

Aunt Winifred, in a rare burst of frigid malice. 'Not before the boy,' said Aunt Brigid, and gave me a sweet from the shop, before shooing me outdoors. Then one evening on the way home from school I stopped in to pray for my many sins before the altar where I served Mass on Sundays. Something in a side altar made me turn: our senior mistress was splayed, with spread-eagled, imploring arms, before the Twelfth Station, Christ Crucified. Her blonde hair flooded her shoulders, and she was sobbing; she did not notice me, so I tiptoed away, dumbfounded by such extravagance. She was beautiful, far more beautiful than my aunt; was she bad like me?

I spent only three years at Garvaghey School, and I cried when I was taken away, for at that age every detail is writ large: to change schools is to change worlds, and I was already attuned to the rules. I did not dare sit beside Mary at Garvaghey School but accepted the partners I was given, mainly girls, the mingling of the sexes seeming to be part of the policy of the school. There was a nice little Protestant girl I sat beside during drawing class but her nose was upturned, she wore glasses, and she was very serious.

While the senior girls blossomed out of reach: plump little Dympna MacGirr, who was supposed to be already courting, her sister Aileen, whose long hair flowed down her shoulders. One wet day, she stood by the school stove drying it; now and again she would shake out its fragrant coils, unaware of my silent adoration, only a desk away. It was as natural as a mare tossing her mane and, indeed, when one of our horses broke loose one evening as we were plodding home from school, I made a big show of taming the animal down for her benefit. But when I found myself behind Aileen in Kelly's shop, I was tongue-tied.

Then the Schools Inspector called, and the prize children were put through their paces. On the junior side, Mary Kelly was to play Little Red Riding Hood and I was the Big Bad Wolf. I danced around her, licking my fangs, delighted with the idea of gobbling her up, neat bonnet, raffia basket and all. No matter if I got slain at the end by the clumsy hatchet of Gus; I had been seen by everyone holding Mary in my arms, and I rose from the dead to stand beside her at the end, while the whole school applauded.

But even amateur wolves fall sick and in my second year at Garvaghey School I came down with a bad cold that turned into a fever. I thrived on fantasy for a while; one of the older children had died that summer, a hefty girl who had spent the whole day in the unaccustomed heat of a blazing sun, and collapsed among the sheaves. We followed the coffin to the old graveyard, and for weeks afterwards we whispered about the mystery of death, bones, worms and ghosts, the terror of being buried alive. But after a few days, the novelty of dying died off; despite the books piled high on my eiderdown. I waited for one of my schoolfriends to come and visit me: I waited for Mary.

She didn't come, she didn't even send one of her awful brothers. And the boys across the way couldn't come; they weren't often in our house, though I slipped into theirs. By the end of the month I was allowed up part of the time, and was hungry for a visitor. It was then that my younger aunt came to announce that I had one, and that it was a girl. Pyjama warm, I hung over the banisters, hoping to greet Mary. But it wasn't her; it was someone else.

At the bottom of our class there was a heavy, nondescript girl from a small labourer's cottage back in the hills; I think her father was a road worker. I wasn't sure of her name because none of us spoke to her, neither the rough nor the politer children. It was Ellen, perhaps, and she had short cropped hair and large obedient eyes, like a waiting spaniel. She had shared a bench with me briefly and made some excuse to speak to me about all the books I read but I brushed her off. Her plainness embarrassed me and, besides, the self-centredness of childhood does not easily allow for the simple fact that others may be feeling the same emotions as oneself, craving for friendship, for love, to escape from the loneliness, the confusion and fears of growing up.

But there she was in the front room of our house, speaking to my younger aunt, and showing her something, slowly and silently. I couldn't see what it was, through the rungs of the stairs, but it was bound to be something horrible, for her family had no money. What a pity it wasn't Mary of the swinging pigtails, with something bright and new from their shop! I would have raced down to see *her*; why hadn't she come?

My aunt climbed the stairs slowly to where I lay petulantly across the bed. She told me that a little schoolmate was waiting for me. A little schoolmate, a little playmate — how I loathed the expressions! I told her that I didn't know her, had never played with her, hardly spoken to her, even when she sat beside me. She was dismal, a real ugly duckling.

'But won't you speak to her?' said my aunt gravely. 'She walked a long way, from Altcloghfin.'

'I don't know her. I don't want to know her.'

My aunt tried again, more slowly.

'But she brought you a present. She wanted to give you a present, she said, because you were away from school and she missed you, and heard that you were sick.'

'I don't want her old present.'

Through the banisters I could see the girl dully waiting — perhaps even hearing our conversation upstairs, if she dared eavesdrop. There was no way I could acknowledge her visit; it was too embarrassing: I would be a laughing stock with all sides for associating with someone like that, whom even the other girls shunned. She was too slow-witted to play most games, rapt in a kind of sleep-walking dream of her own, away from the brisk rattle of camogie sticks, or skipping.

'Tell her to go away. Tell her I'm still sick. I'm, I'm *contagious*!'

And so down she went, down the stairs, and I saw her speak to Ellen. The little girl said nothing, but placed her present on the parlour table, then left. When my aunt turned from seeing her through the door, I saw something very strange: my aunt's head was bowed, as if she was praying, or crying. What under Heaven was wrong?

A safe time afterwards, I crept downstairs to inspect the object which had caused all the unpleasantness. It was a shoebox and in it lay a small, brittle, celluloid doll. Not a fancy doll, with long yellow eyelashes, which cried, or closed its eyes if it was laid down, like the big one her father had given Mary at Christmas. No, it was a frightful little object, like a juju from one of my adventure stories, made of some nasty pink material. It couldn't have cost more than a few shillings from some place like Woolworth's.

Was that all she could afford? In a corner of the box was a little note, badly spelt, which ran:

FOR MY SIC BOYFRIEND
THE DOLL I LUV

As I read it, each word, each laborious letter burnt with shame into my arrogant, precious little spirit. I had met true love, and because of the shabbiness of its dress, had spurned it from my door.

The Limits of Innocence

It was his especial pride that he was always the first, and some-times the only one, to answer in class. Auburn-haired and inquisitive, he gathered knowledge without difficulty, passing from class to class as though school were only another sort of game. Standing in a sullen line by the blackboard, the country children swung their heads in bewilderment as the agile little schoolmaster questioned and abruptly demanded:

'The Black Country, where is it? What is Sheffield famous for? The chief industries of Belfast? The chief rivers of Spain?'

Then, meeting no answer, the schoolteacher turned:

'Surely somebody knows! You, Leo Donaghy, what are the chief rivers of Spain?'

'The Douro, the Tagus, the Ebro, the Guadiana and Gua-dalquivir.'

In his mind's eye he saw five silver rivers race across a rocky tableland, and wondered why anyone should find history or geography difficult when they presented such strange and exciting images of places unseen, as in a story book. And yet for the other children school was only a form of unshunned prison, a dumbfounding purgatory from which they gladly escaped in the end to the relatively simple work of the fields. The country people marvelled at his alertness, saying, 'He's a bright lad, that', though half convinced from their own experience that such learning was only a useless burden, to be shed when one left school to toil and moil long days on the cramped stubborn fields of a hill farm. 'It's grand to be a scholar if you're going to be a clergyman or a schoolmaster, but what use is it herding cows, or driving a plough?' was their attitude, dutifully passed on to their children, to the total exasperation of the master.

Nevertheless, they had a great respect for intelligence, a

bright transitory ornament, and in school Leo found himself called again and again to help others avoid punishment, especially when the schoolmaster was in an angry mood.

* * *

He did not know, then, when he noticed her first, a large torpid girl standing on the line with the third class, her head bent, her fingers fumbling on a jotter with a stub of gnawed pencil.

Concentrating on his work, following the squeak of chalk outlining a problem on the blackboard, he had little time for anything else, until one day when she leant across his shoulder to copy the answer to a sum, and he felt the fragrance of her arms, the peach-like bloom of her cheek touching his, ever so slightly. He felt puzzled, and could not remember what to do next in his work; it seemed pointless to him. It was early spring, with flowers bursting into colour on the contrary rock garden; he was moved by her presence as though by a breath of warm air flowing into the schoolroom through an open window.

From that day forward, he watched her, quietly, and without being noticed, hardly even realising his own absorption. She was a year older than he was, though in a lower class. Tall, his own height, her brown hair hung limply down her back in pigtails. Her temples were rounded, and in the slight warm dent between them stray hairs glinted. She moved slowly as though in a constant dream, and even when the schoolmaster questioned her, she answered with the disinterest of a sleepwalker.

'You, Sally Hanlon, do you know?'

'What, sir?'

'Did you hear the question or were you sleeping?'

'No, sir.'

'Do you ever do any work at all?'

'Yes, sir.'

Then he saw her cherry red palms tilted for the cane, coming down sharply on the long fingers. She never cried, but wrung her hands mechanically, as though washing them, or pressed them against the cool stuff of her dress. The schoolmaster seemed to have some special reason for disliking her; he punished her so often that her hands showed welts where the blood had clotted. The boy wondered why anyone should wish to hurt someone so beautiful; it seemed like a sacrilege. He offered to help her, with some humility, hardly knowing how to speak to her, or what about.

'It's easy. Honest it is, I'll show you.'

She smiled back at him as he babbled in his efforts to explain. She had a self-absorbed smile that bent the corners of her lips and made shadows around her brown eyes.

In the playground at midday she stood apart from the other girls, hardly bothering to join in the shrill camogie game waged on the patch of ground before the school. They, in turn, resented her quiet, watchful air, the fact that companionship hardly seemed necessary to her. It was as though she was waiting for something; he did not know what.

A certain unspoken intimacy grew up between them. Although she was in a class below him, they shared certain lessons; by accident he found himself placed in the desk directly in front of her. She said little, but now and again she bent over his shoulder, so that he could feel the slight pressure of her breast, and the subtle lightness of her breath.

That whole spring he worked harder than ever; he was preparing for a scholarship examination that would take him away from the valley. But though he had very few hours to himself he was completely happy, in a wild and exhilarating way that he had never known before. After working all evening he would walk across the fields, delighting in the smell of rain on the hawthorn hedges, the damp musk of leaves and ferns in a corner of a ditch. All these sights and sounds, sharp and releasing on the senses as physical pain, were somehow mingled for him with the knowledge of her working behind him daily in school. His days were dictated by a new rhythm: the knowledge and adoration of beauty.

* * *

He spoke to her only once outside class, lacking both courage and opportunity. It was the following autumn; there was a choir practice in the chapel in preparation for October devotions, and he took a shortcut down by the river. He saw her coming, a brown beret on her hair, the slender legs moving under a brown coat. He hardly knew what to say to her, she seemed so assured and self-contained. With great nervousness he spoke of the day in school.

'He was very cross today.'

She looked at him; her dark steady gaze made his face redden.

'Why is he so angry with you?'

She thought deeply, eyes on the ground. 'I never have time to do my exercises.'

'Why don't you? I always do, I could help you.'

'I think they're silly, and besides I haven't time.'

He was silent, not understanding very well. 'Do you have to work so hard at home?'

'I'm always out late,' she said, with a curious shyness as though confiding an important secret. 'And he knows that.'

'And how does he know?'

She was silent. He pretended to know the mystery which kept her from staying in the house and working. His face was tense with the effort of sympathy, for he realised that she must have something very important to occupy her all the evenings, something more important than a childish thing like housework, and something certainly which he for all his supposed brightness could not easily understand. It was part of the mystery of her loneliness in school, the heady perfume of her body, the vicious way in which the schoolmaster showed his dislike and the girls pointed their gossiping, jealous fingers.

'I'll do your homework for you if you like,' he said gallantly.

She did not bother to answer, but walked closely beside him, so that he was almost drunk with the warmth of her presence. Across the river lay a football field; a few boys were punting around a heavy ball, and there came an occasional shout. The river gurgled quietly over silvered stones, and in the shadowy half silence of the autumn evening, with the smell of dead leaves and bark in the air, he could hear her soft breathing. Crossing the bridge halfway down the path their bodies touched. Suddenly bold, he took her hand.

'That's very nice of you,' she said.

'What?'

'To try to help me. But I don't mind being slapped.'

Her fingertips were warm and she moved them against his with a delicate circular movement that made his palm itch, until he felt himself crushing her hand without restraint.

'O-oh,' she said, wincing.

'Did I hurt you?'

They stood facing each other at the curve in the path, hidden from the main road and the chapel, under a high elm tree.

'No,' she whispered. Again, their bodies touched, and he saw the lovely head within reach of his fingertips. She leant forward, and he felt his arms around her, and for a strange moment they stood, hearing a bird cry above their heads in the elm tree.

'Silly Billy kissing Nelly.'

Four small children, two boys and two girls, were dancing at the end of the path, calling and chanting.

'Silly Billy kisses Nelly.'

Abashed, they separated, and hurried on; there was a slight flush on her cheeks, but their fingers were laced.

As he sang in the choir that evening, and all the evenings of the following October, the young voices rising in the cold roof of the chapel, he thought of her, and when the incense fumed across the rails at Benediction, he could think only of her image, and not of the coloured statue of the Virgin before the altar. Joining in the Litany of the Divine Praises and the sequence of adoration in the words of the Litany to the Blessed Virgin, it was as if he prayed to her, seeing her move, young and warm-bodied, in the background of his mind.

Again and again, at home or in school, he tasted that single kiss on his lips — the warm tenderness of it, which his physical innocence worshipped like the receiving of a sacrament. Though he continued to watch her in class, and occasionally saw her impassive gaze answer his, they never spoke alone again; walking home in the evenings he heard the boys joking about her, with a strange laughter that he could not understand. Once, one of them came over to him, with an air of coarse excitement.

'Weren't you seen with Sally Hanlon down by the Waterside Road?'

'What do you mean?'

The boys laughed and leaped wildly, flinging their school-bags in the air.

'Was it good?'

'What do you mean?'

They hooted, and he turned his head away, keeping his be-wilderment and doubt to himself. But he could not help overhearing their stories, coloured with loud and awkward oaths.

'And there they were stretched out in the feckin' grass, and his leg over hers like a bull trying to mount a cow....'

Another time, in the boarding house of the schoolmaster, where he sometimes called in the evenings for special scholar-ship lessons, he heard someone say:

'That one. No wonder she hasn't time for school. She takes all her lessons in the dark.'

* * *

The months passed slowly, with autumn merging into the frost-bright days of winter, when the birds were quiet and the bare thorn hedges crisp with rime. It was his last year in the school, and the thought of going away filled him with a certain melancholy.

Before Christmas there was the bustle of preparing the an-nual school concert, organised by the teachers with the help of the parish priest. As head of the senior class he was to assist in producing a short play. Shy himself, he yet knew exactly what others should do when they took the stage. He coached them with a firmness and certainty that surprised even himself.

When the night came, the two cloakrooms, which had been changed into dressing rooms, were full of excited children; the costumes for the play had arrived only that morning by bus, and there were 'Ooh's of wonder as the glittering dresses and soldiers' uniforms were drawn out.

He had been deputed to act as steward, and in his new suit and white collar he felt rather important, ushering people to their seats, or rushing to the door of one of the dressing rooms.

'Hurry up there. We've no time. The priest's here.'

When the concert began, he watched from a side doorway. The first part of the programme consisted of children singing, mainly to please their parents, who made up the bulk of the audience. The play made up the second half. During the interval he felt very restless and nervous. Now that the green makeshift curtains were about to open, and knowing that she was to play the part of the fairy godmother in the first act, he felt afraid in case anything should go wrong.

When she appeared on the stage, only for a brief moment, gliding mysteriously from the wings in order to grant the wishes of a sleeping child, he saw that her hair had been loosened from the pigtails, and fell around her shoulders in a great mass. She had a circlet on her head, with a single star shining in the front. As the curtain came down on the first act, he moved towards the girls' dressing room, hardly conscious of what he was doing. He knocked on the door, gently. There was no answer. Entering, he saw her standing before a mirror, hair still loose, flowing down her back. She turned in surprise, and he saw that her dress had been unbuttoned from the shoulders down; he could see, peeping above the thin white undergarment, the tops of her breasts.

On the stage a bell rang sharply for the beginning of the second act. She adjusted her dress with a quick movement, and came towards him. 'Could we go out for a while?' he stammered. The request seemed idiotic but she did not appear to mind. He caught her hand and with a quick look round to see if anyone was watching, they ran out through the door into the school playground. The sharp iron railings on the top of the wall and the worn stone of the playground patch shone under moonlight.

'Look up,' she said.

The cold procession of the northern lights filled a part of the sky. He looked for a while and then said:

'I prefer looking at you.'

She laughed at his earnestness. He could see her body moving under the transparent shimmering dress of the fairy godmother, as though even such delicate stuff hindered her natural freedom. She continued to look upwards, as if willing to lose herself for the moment in watching the glittering immensities of the night sky.

'Come on,' he said.

'Where?'

'I have an idea.' Filled with an extraordinary spirit of adventure, he took her hand, moving towards the dark shrubbery which grew on the hillock surrounding the school. This sandy contorted patch, where bushes and shrubs dug their twisted roots into the earth, was part of the playground, and even during the daytime a dark and dew-damp underworld, with secret hiding places, long grasses where the children searched for pignuts or, in winter, slopes for sliding. A thorn tree sent drops of moisture tingling down the backs of their necks.

'Where are we going?'

'Anywhere. Are you afraid?'

She pressed slightly against him but did not answer.

'Come on. We can see the school from the top.' He pulled her by the hand as high as they could go, laughing as they tumbled over the roots that sprawled like snakes across the path. He held a swinging briar aside to prevent her dress from being torn, until, parting the screen of heavy leaves, they fought their heads clear of the sour-sweet-smelling tunnels of the shrubbery. Below them the school lay, a good deal smaller now in its miniature valley, with moonlight on the tiles of the roof and lamplight pouring from all the windows.

They stood together watching. The night smell, compounded of leaves and earth, was dense in his nostrils; in some way it reminded him of the girl at his side.

'Are you sure they won't miss us?'

'We've lots of time. They haven't even ended yet, and then they'll have to clear up.'

'Look, there's the Parochial House.'

The large yellow-brick house of the parish priest lay on the other side of the slope. The top of the hillock marked the boundary of the school playground; beyond a barbed-wire fence lay the grounds of the house, with mist swirling over the shadowy mass of a plantation. There was a rigidly enforced rule that none of the children ever crossed into these fields to play or even to chase a lost ball.

'Could we cross it?'

'We daren't,' she said.

In his nervous way he was more urgent and daring than she. He pushed through the strands of wire in a flash, and then held them apart for her to follow. She climbed cautiously through, lifting her dress with one hand. For a second he saw the white flesh above her knee exposed.

'Hurry up.'

Then they were both through, and ran breathless away from the fence through the wet high grass. She was laughing and he pretended to chase her, until they found themselves on the other side of the field where the outskirts of the pine plantation cast an aromatic shadow, and the giant trees strode away, ghostlike and glittering, into the darkness towards the river.

A frog ran with electric leaps through the grass. She screamed slightly and stumbled, falling to her knees. He bent down beside her.

'Are you hurt?' he asked tenderly.

He touched her shoulders with his hands, gently and yet with great excitement. He knelt down beside her and kissed her, feeling her breast against his, soft against firm.

'You shouldn't do that,' she said softly.

'I can't help it. You're so beautiful.'

She hid her head, turning it slightly away from his.

'You shouldn't say things like that. Nobody ever does.'

'But it's true.'

He touched the frail mist of hair above her ears. He was almost afraid to touch the rippling lustrous mass of hair; it was as if he would lose his wrists in it. A sheep came stumbling towards them where they lay on the grass. It sniffed suspiciously and then took to its heels.

'Look,' she said, laughing. 'Aren't sheep silly?'

He made as if to kiss her again.

'Behave yourself.'

There was a note in her voice that he had never heard before, as though she were pretending to be an adult, and yet was half ashamed of the pretence. Suddenly she pulled his head down towards hers again, shifting her body so that it touched his full-length. A shudder of feeling passed through him, so intense that he did not know whether it was good or evil, pain or ecstasy.

'Bad boy,' she whispered. 'What were you doing in the dressing room?'

He was apologetic. 'Honestly, I'm sorry.'

She laughed. 'Am I so ugly then?'

'Oh Lord, no!' he said, in a hushed voice as though speaking of something sacred. His innocent awareness, nearer to adoration than love, must have touched her; the harsh uncertain note left her voice.

'You're so funny,' she said. 'And really nice.'

'Am I?' he asked with surprise. He didn't know whether to be pleased or not.

'You are,' she said. 'I wish others were as kind as you.' She spoke as though trying to release some sorrow that he could not understand.

He moved his fingers around the column of her throat, touching the front of her dress. It was still partly open; in her hurry she had left the top undone.

'You'll catch cold,' he said.

'Button it for me.'

His hands moved over the substance of the dress, searching for the buttons. He felt her tense, her shoulders tighten, as he fumbled, conscious of the small mounds of the twin breasts under the cloth. Raising her shoulders with a slight moan she reached down, shrugging back the dress and the thin undergarment until the upper part of her body lay bare on the grass. In silent wonder he touched the flesh of her side, pale as buttermilk, with the veins delicately blue under the skin. It was the first time he had seen the body of a girl even partly naked. With sudden heat and daring he touched her breasts. His hands, moving over the skin, had learnt a new and secret tenderness, as though the nerves under the fingertips were bare. The crisp nipples arched under his touch like tiny spikes. He almost swooned with excitement and terror.

They lay in the grass without moving for a few minutes. A star disintegrated in an arc down the sky. Her body was motionless under his now quiet caressing touch. He half closed his eyes, feeling the rhythmic movement of her torso beneath his hands, smelling the acrid fragrance of her hair against his mouth. The side of his face was growing wet with dew.

'We'd better go,' she said suddenly, sitting up. Her voice was soft and she looked more openly at him. He helped her to her feet and she stood combing her hair.

'Where's the band?'

He found it lying in the grass, the cheap crinkled star winking up at him. He helped her to pull it down upon her forehead, and drew a few scattered twigs from her hair. Then he took her hand.

'Come on,' she said.

Hand in hand, they walked across the field, away from the smell and shadow of the pines. They scrambled through the barbed-wire fence and stood again on the crest of the hillock, looking down at the school. The lights were still on; the concert was only ending. She kicked a tuft of grass, moodily. The tip of her shoe was wet and gleaming.

'Do you like me still?' she asked.

'I love you,' he said. He had never used the word before, but he was sure he knew what it meant.

They moved downwards through the dank windings of the shrubbery. Stones slid under their feet, and with her moist palm in his, the boy felt no longer doubtful. He whistled lightly with assurance and joy. The steam of their breaths mingled in a loose skein on the night air. He had come to understand something of mystery, and yet, miraculously, it remained mystery for him still.

1952

Above Board

When my cousin Agnes came up from the South for the summer holidays I suddenly became very popular. She was at a
convent school, but in her sixteenth year she had sprouted, with
all the signs of young womanhood. I was uneasy about the
change, which I dimly understood; after all, I had known the
precocious girls of Glencull School, but that sort of thing was
not discussed in our house, and to have a sleepwalking young
beauty under our own roof was something new.

It also changed our relationship. She and her younger
brother were my best friends, but her change made him very
angry: he hissed at her at every meal and silently kicked her
under the table. The older people ate at another table, when
they were together at our house, and her older brothers ignored
the drama as beneath them, which it was. Sometimes I got a
hefty kick on the shin myself when young Seán missed his
target.

Meanwhile she drew near to me, as if she needed me, which
was very flattering. She came with me to drive the cows to the
mountain pastures in the morning, leaving a sulking Seán
behind. And then we would strike out into the high bog, cart
tracks sunk so deep that you were invisible between the high
banks, the mystery of MacCrystal's Glen with its twisted thorns
and banks of prickly yellow whin. Sometimes we stopped for a
rest, and we would share a bar of chocolate, which I had saved
from my wartime rations for her. We sat side by side on a
spread raincoat, talking, usually about love, who we would
meet; and marry, of course.

She had already introduced this theme, a year earlier, when
I went South. I had got off the bus in Longford, and begun to
haul my suitcase towards her home, but there was no sign of

her, although she was supposed to meet me with her bicycle. Finally Agnes appeared, dusting her skirt, and wheeled the bicycle from a gateway. She had used the excuse of meeting me to spend an hour with a young clerk from the town, called 'Tosh' Ryan. She showed me his letters, four or five scrawled pages, full of vague compliments. She said they might help me if I was in love, to know how to write to please girls, but I was sure I could do better. 'Bosh' Ryan seemed a better name for his style!

Another swain was introduced to me, a turf driver from Castlepollard. He came rattling past the door every day, lashing the poor donkey to give some impression of speed. We met him in the snug of a public house once. He bought me a lemonade while he drank a pint, and Agnes and he stared at each other. He had reddish-brown crinkly hair hanging over his eyes in a quiff, which he kept smoothing back. I thought he looked terribly vulgar, no class, but I sipped my free lemonade and said nothing.

I doubt if much happened on these meetings; kissing, cuddling, and muffled endearments from love stories were all that were permitted to the better-class, convent-bred girl. I was more afraid for my cousin in my own home area, where I knew the score and she didn't. Whatever about fancy letters from town clerks, I knew what the boys around Garvaghey were thinking — hadn't we played under Rarogan Hill, making drawings of women in the sand? Every copy of *Lilliput*, with its pictures of naked women tastefully posed between sailing swans and ripening fruit, was devoured with an avidity we rarely brought to our lessons.

So when big Shamus Lynch began to lumber behind us as we drove out the cows, I managed to drive him away. Big Shamus had a dull square face and a dogged manner, with the leglifting attitudes of a canine in heat. But, despite a head crammed with bad thoughts, he was bashful, so I just told him I would tell his mother on him. She was the rival of my Aunt Brigid for holiness in the parish, kneeling long after everyone had left the chapel, praying and sighing to herself: 'Mother of Jesus, help us'. As well she might sigh, since she was so pregnant at her wedding that she gave birth to big Shamus on the side of the road on her way home from the feast.

Or so I heard. You must understand that I was not part of all this interest in sex, except as a bystander. My maiden aunts never mentioned it, and I knew that I would be going to a better school, maybe even to become a priest! No one knew about my secret yearnings to be as bad as the boldest of them. If that was what was wanted, of course — my real inclination was towards chivalry but it didn't seem the way love was practised in my home territory.

So I didn't want that sort of game associated with my lovely cousin upon whom, in return for her confidences, I began to lavish my longings. We took long walks; heads together, we read the same books, from Zane Grey to Leslie Charteris.

I saw myself as a knight who would stand guard over her, come what may. The expeditions I planned, to the pictures in Omagh, or a climb to some secret place, were partly invented to please her; poor Seán tried to tag along, but soon dropped away when we barely spoke to him, or walked too fast for his shorter stride.

The last intruder I had to drive off was Austin, a foxy-haired young fellow a few years older than myself, who knew more than was good for him, and already boasted about having got the knickers off several girls. Since my cousin Agnes had arrived he had become very friendly with me, by the way, but I could see his play coming.

One afternoon he came down towards us, whistling, as we were starting to drive out the cows. Luckily, his father called him away, but a few days afterwards he slithered down a hedge so abruptly that he startled one of the cows, who shot off through a gap in the hedge. He shot off after it, but the damage was done: he had presented himself more as a rustler than a useful cowhand. I was able to go on calmly pursuing my conversation with Agnes, who steadfastly ignored him, having already been fed scarifying reports from me about his grossness.

We were using each other, I suppose: I was acting as a shield for her, and she flattered me by showing so much attention to a youngster like myself, whom the older girls ignored. And slowly I fell in love with my sense of her; not the breasts and thighs I and the other boys discussed hungrily, but a real young woman, who asked me to sit beside her on the edge of her blue school raincoat, shared my chocolate, accepted my sweets, and let her long, dark, fragrant hair fall across my face.

It was summer, of course, and what few flowers we knew were in blossom. The foxglove thrust its red fingers at us on the way to the upland pastures, and irises showed their yellow flags in bottom meadows. There were more intimate sights: the minute blue of forget-me-not, the daisy's tiny heart, a shock of bluebells sheltering under a tree. We were not strong on flowers, but their perfume mingled with our wanderings, and in the high bog, as the wind combed the heather, there was a constant, sweet scent, a silent sound of heatherbells. We found blaeberries or fraughans, the blue berry of the bogs, which we smeared on each other's faces, laughing all the while. We were discovering a little about life at the same time as nature herself was coming alive; although we carefully said nothing about our feelings for each other, it was a sweet exchange.

Then one admirer made an outflanking move. He was Manus Donnelly, the young shopboy from the local grocer's. A sheepish young fellow with flaxen hair, he had not attracted my attention much since he didn't play football for the Garvaghey team. His only claim to fame so far was that he had cut the top off his finger with the new Berkel bacon slicer; I was in the shop at the time and saw him holding up the reddening finger in surprise. Then he touched it and the nail fell off, onto the counter, before the waiting customers. Mrs Lynch fainted and Manus himself had to be helped away, before the doctor came.

That a fool like that should be wooing my beautiful cousin seemed ludicrous to me, but she appeared to like it. He seemed reluctant to make direct moves, though we spent longer and longer in the shop over some simple message or other. I fumed as he fumbled for topics of conversation: how could anyone stand those long silences? Agnes did not seem to mind, ready to wait as the Calor-gas lamp hissed and other customers came and went.

Then he devised a Trojan Horse, which brought him right inside our house. I don't know if my aunts or her parents were aware of the interest that Agnes was causing: the way boys gaped through the window, came into the post office to buy stamps for non-existent letters, or waited on the roadside to greet us as we went forth on some simple errand — going to the well, or fetching the cows. But then Pa Doherty arrived one night for a card game, with young Manus in tow.

Cards are, or were, a bit like religion in the countryside: you had to welcome the players who chose your house. And Uncle John loved cards, in a mild sort of way, a vice I had never suspected him of. Even my aunts would join in, grumpily at first, because visitors meant a disturbance of the household routine, and making tea for everyone; but they also liked the bit of drama. Bit, indeed, because it was one of the slowest and simplest games in the world: twenty-five for a penny. That it was not being played for purely gambling motives didn't seem to cross their minds, though the obsessions of Pa Doherty were well documented.

Pa, or Pa-trick, lived opposite the church, with his two scraggy spinster sisters. He was a not-so-spry bachelor in his early sixties, a long drip of a man with a straggly moustache, like Mr Gump in my American funny papers. But he had a thing about women, in a harmless sort of way; one was always hearing that Pa was visiting with some new Dulcinea, usually a middle-aged woman whose brothers had suddenly died, leaving her in charge. He was also to be seen at the corner as the school scattered; he never offered sweets to little girls, but he looked sweetly at them. That this wizened rooster should dare to dream, even daydream, of my cousin was something monstrous to me. I joined in the card games from evil motives, whenever I was allowed, hoping to cheat the lovelorn. For he and Manus spent more time looking at Agnes than at the black and red of their playing cards. It made me rage to intercept their lovesick glances as they played wrong cards, missing suits or tricks because they were thinking only of one thing.

After they had been there several weeks in a row, even my elders began to feel the game pall. There was no sharpness in it, and it was clear that young Manus was losing part of his salary every evening, playing as if he were sleepwalking. No matter how small the stakes, they added up, and the winners felt abashed at taking such easy pickings, whatever the reason. Besides, people were beginning to talk, and we became dimly aware that somehow or other it had to stop.

So what I decided to do to bring them to their senses was not punished as it might otherwise have been. Time after time, when a card was dropped, a bright red heart or a dark cluster of clubs, I dived in search of it, still small enough to go down inside the forest of legs and retrieve the missing rectangle of cardboard. I got to know that strange world down there, under the table: the solid knees of my Uncle John, the skinny ones of Pa Doherty, the flannels of Manus Donnelly, the demure convent-pleated skirt of my cousin, the longer, warm aprons of my aunts, like Indian tents.

A few times, when I slid down quickly, I noticed that something was going on. Pa Doherty's knee would abruptly withdraw from near that of my cousin, or I would find Manus's foot out of its shoe, and wandering, also in the vicinity of Agnes. I decided to do something about it, in that strange half-lit world of knees and legs and ankles. One night when I was down I tied the shoeless foot of Manus to the nudging knee of Pa Doherty, using a length of string I had smuggled down with me.

The result was spectacular enough to satisfy any of my fictional heroes. Pa put down his pipe, which issued clouds of acrid, grey smoke, and decided to cross his legs, to bring him luck perhaps. The binder twine — I had not stinted in my subterranean operation — lifted the foot of Manus which landed in the lap of Agnes. She rose with a modest expostulation, and the table rose with her, or rather tilted. Seeing her rise, Pa also rose, like a true gentleman, and the deck of cards slid into Aunt Mary's lap, Kings, Queens, Jacks and all, to be followed slowly, the table now bounding and bucking as though possessed, by the teapot, which disappeared with a slow and stately motion over the edge, onto Uncle John's trousers. He was a quiet man by nature, but the roar he let out as the scalding contents of the big teapot — it had just been wet for the nightcap — landed across his fork would have done justice to Coote's bull.

The great thing was that through hauling and pulling, the string broke, and no one ever really knew what happened. I slid down under the table like lightning to untie the remaining knots and slip the evidence into my pocket, or up my gansey, whichever was quicker. The wreckage I confronted when I came up was very satisfactory: everyone wore a startled and strained air, as if they had swallowed a hedgehog. The parents of Agnes were not overly protective but they had realised that in some way their daughter was in danger, and that even a senior citizen like Pa was not above suspicion. As for young Manus, he was beetroot with embarrassment and loss.

Nothing was formally said, but they never came back. I was sorry for Manus: although I could not bear his lovelorn, gawky looks, he was less menacing than some of my cousin's suitors. But there was something pathetic about him wooing a serious girl, someone so foolish that he could cut off his finger with a bacon slicer! He had taken to wearing a little red sheath over it, which made people ask about it so that he could bare the stump to admiring eyes. But it didn't sound like bravery to me — he was far from the front line when he got that wound. As for Pa Doherty, he had brought out all the amorous bigot in me. He was a gentle soul, gentle to the point of simple-mindedness, and whatever feeling he may have had about girls during his younger days had been strangled by his situation. He was, in effect, married to his sisters, two renowned churchgoers, and already fulfilling that mystic role of being 'the man about the house'. I can see him now, leaning over the gatepost as school broke. Were his watery blue eyes and drooping moustaches moist with lust, as he gazed at the young MacGirrs and Johnsons and Kavanaghs? I doubt it: looking at them, deep down in him, his distant youth stirred, like a fish lost in a pool who had once heard tell of the ocean.

Sugarbush, I Love You So

It was after Christmas in Tyrone and my pal Frank Carney said he would bring us all to the New Year's dance in Strabane. There was little Phil Barrell, who hated college boys like myself, there was Hughie the hairdresser, with his gleaming Brylcreemed hair, who was mad for the women, and kept touching himself absentmindedly, there was my boxing pal Gerry Cullen whose proud boast was that he had double-jointed fists that he could crack like pistol shots. It was as unappetising a gang of louts or local scruff as our little town could manage, more like an invading party of Visigoths than a group of Catholic young men.

Among us, a rare enough occurrence, was a young girl home on her holidays from Scotland. I found myself talking to her as we drove slowly along the fogbound river. She had a job working in Glasgow as a clippie, or conductor, on one of the city buses, and was therefore better able to pay her way than any of us. She said very little on the drive up, probably intimidated by our boisterous bravado, our show of worldliness. And when I came to the dance hall I ignored her, eagerly casing the local talent, who had the advantage of living far from our home. After all, she was small, sturdy, freckled, not obviously pretty, and probably from the back-lane houses where my grandmother had once collected the rents, a member of a class I was not supposed to associate with, who had never progressed beyond primary school. Class was not something clearly defined in the country and the small towns, but it was very potent nonetheless, all the more so for being largely unspoken: tuppence ha'penny looking down on tuppence.

Strabane that night did not seem to offer any answer to my vague romantic dreams; after the long slow drive beside the River Foyle, the dance itself was anticlimactic, the music tired, the girls listless. So I turned back before the Intermission to give the young girl who had travelled with us a duty dance, a courtesy I did not always honour. To my surprise, it was more than a pleasure. Her body moulded sweetly into mine, as if we had been made for each other. I tried all my youthful masher's steps, so carefully learnt in Dublin, and she responded to them all. Usually when a dance ended, couples eased uneasily apart, but she remained close to me, her arm round my shoulder, her breast and thigh warmly against mine, before we swung into the next dance. It was a hit tune of the period, which still sways in my mind: *Sugarbush, I love you so, I won't ever let you go.* By the time the Intermission came, we were dancing cheek to cheek, and during the break she followed me outside.

The car was large, a hackney, and we settled into its back seat, snug as a double bed. The fog was still thick, with the street lamps burning through it. This time there was no calculation, no slow persuasion; she was just eager for sex. To my astonishment, I found myself doing naturally what I had spent so many hours dreaming of; entwined in easy ecstasy with a willing companion. I did not have to waste precious minutes on languorous Hollywood kisses — she knew what she wanted. Nor was there any need for the ritual fight through layers of clothing, as she loosened her skirt and bra to welcome me into the warm haven of her body. There was nothing extravagant or exaggerated about it, just natural desire naturally expressed; she wanted to go the whole way.

After our first bout, we sat talking and smoking Wild Woodbine cigarettes, like grown-ups, listening to the muffled music of the dance band, the Melody Aces. She told me that she had learnt a lot in Scotland, that the life on the buses was tough, but no tougher than at home, where her father had begun to bother her. The Scots were rough, but their hearts were easily touched. There was a kind of working-class solidarity of knowledge; the other girls on the buses taught her about contraception, the times of the month that were nearly safe, and where to go if things went wrong. She only had boys when she knew or thought things would be all right, and I had been lucky enough to fall on that period. She was a bit shocked that a college boy like myself knew so little, but it did not prevent her drawing me back into another embrace. We managed to get back to the hall for the last round-up, but I did not dance with anyone else.

The atmosphere in the car on the way back was more than awkward. My pal the driver did not take sides; we were old hunting companions, and he was glad to see me looking so happy. But the others were very uneasy. Hughie the hairdresser shifted his hands in the darkness as the girl and I nestled together; it sounded as though he were masturbating, and yet he had barely spoken to her on the way up because in that infinitesimally graded class system of a social limbo like Fentown, he had mentally spurned her as being below even him, and therefore socially invisible. Little Phil was outraged, and kept muttering about how college boys thought they could get away with anything. Gerry Cullen was cracking his fists and announcing, 'Good man, John,' every time we kissed. That large black hackney, sailing along the fogbound river in the early morning, was as dense with class consciousness as a Proustian *salon*, but with everyone looking down, except the girl.

The car came to Fentown. Frank cheerfully asked me in to have a few slices of the big cooked Christmas ham, but I hesitated. The girl waited quietly behind me while Frank went in, and came out with a small parcel of sandwiches: 'I see what's on your minds, but I can't leave the car open all night, the old fellow would find out, and that would be the end of our wee excursions. I wish you luck, anyway,' he said, watching our disgruntled companions march off down the road. As he closed the door I thought furiously of the few possibilities we had. Our own side door was open, but we could shelter there only briefly, as our rustling might alert my family, and my new friend lived in the smallest of small houses, and probably slept with another member of the family, aunt or sister.

It was then I thought of Fentown's main claim to glory, the Horse Tram. This contraption was a two-storey carriage used to draw passengers from Fentown station to Fentown Junction, one mile out along the tracks. It was the only one of its kind in Ireland, and indeed, as far as we were concerned, the world. It was old-fashioned, with well-cushioned seats and a curved wrought-iron rail leading to the balcony. Hand in hand, we found our way down to the station, and the empty tram. Side by side, we ate our sandwiches contentedly; then, spreading our overcoats like blankets, wrapped ourselves up on one of the benches, to resume where we had left off.

We were both young, full of ardour and energy, but although we went at it a long time, falling back only to start again, we eventually fell asleep in each other's arms. When we awoke there was a gentle swaying motion underneath us: it was morning, and the Fentown Horse Tram was on its way out to meet the first train from Enniskillen. In the early dawn, the driver had harnessed his horse with all the somnolence of habit, unaware that he was carrying people out to meet the train, since he had not seen us board. Sleepy, dishevelled, we prodded each other awake to watch the broad, thickly clothed back of the driver, with his cap like a policeman's uniform. At Fentown Junction he dismounted, and we sheltered in our corner to travel calmly back with the incoming voyagers a little later. Then we parted smartly, although I thought I saw someone watching from the far side of the street. Soon I was snug in my bed, under the Holy Pictures, as if I had never left it.

I slept through the late morning into the afternoon. I felt, or thought I felt, someone at the door, but the house in Fentown was slow to rise; my elder brothers usually lay late and long in bed. But this time I was out to rival them, pleasantly exhausted with the unexpected joys of lovemaking, and not hungry either because of the plentiful sandwiches, slabs of thick, pink, home-cooked ham bordered with white fat and smelling of cloves, a kind offering from my friend Frank. So I descended into that lull between lunch and tea, said hello to my mother in the kitchen, and sauntered out into the twilight for a stroll to St Lawrence's Hall, to play a game of table tennis or billiards in the basement where the respectable young of the town met.

My red-headed middle brother was halfway through a game on one of the green billiard tables. I came over to watch his game and make encouraging noises, but got little change for my support. Indeed, he seemed almost hostile, and I began to have that vague feeling, which I remembered so well from school, that I had done something wrong, in some way I did not understand, offended against some code, offended against the immutable laws of society and God. I thought I had left all that behind when I went to college, but I could see from the snap in his eyes, and his bristling, laconic answers, that as far as he was concerned I had done something. Since he was the smoother of my brothers, a dancer famous for his skills from Belfast to Omagh, and a gambler who had often borrowed from his baby brother, I looked up to him as someone sophisticated in the rules of our small society, who knew the score, so I waited to walk home with him along Main Street, Fentown, Co. Tyrone. He did not seem inclined to speak, but finally did.

'I hear you had a great time last night,' he said sharply.

It took me a while to answer. After all, it was only a few hours ago, and I was still warm from the experience, which I hoped to repeat as soon as possible.

'I suppose you could call it that,' I said. 'I did meet a nice girl, and we got along well.'

He emitted a peculiar sound, derisive, nearly a hoot. 'You know where she comes from, don't you?' As if that explained everything.

I briefly tried my best. 'I think I do, but you know I don't know the town very well. Besides, does it really matter? I thought she was a very nice girl, and a pleasure to meet in a place like this.'

He turned to face me on the street, his jaw rigid with anger. 'Well, you had better not meet her again. Don't even *you* know that you can't slut on your own doorstep?'

How had he learnt? Probably from Phil Barrell who had kept a jealous watch during the night, probably masturbating at the thought of our pleasure. Or had old Dick, the station guard, finally woken up to our presence? He was a Protestant, as with almost all public jobs, and would probably be glad to report any Papish misdemeanour. Anyway, someone had told, and the damage was done: my brother had dropped the portcullis to protect the morals of our home from any low-life adventure; I had offended against the rules of society and family by having to do with a girl from the wrong side of the tram tracks. I weighed her easy warmth against such wrath, and, alas, gave in.

She sent some pencilled messages through her baby sister. I received them at the door and then turned inside. I saw her once or twice on the other side of the street, and she smiled at me and waved urgently, but I passed heavily on. I did not have to suffer my own cowardice too long — by the end of the holidays she had lifted anchor and sailed back to Glasgow, her new and hopefully more generous home.

Pilgrim's Pad

I

If she does not come, my heart stands still:
Instead of summer, winter in a bound.
And if she comes, my golden girl,
Where do I stand? I die as well.

It was a makeshift notebook of the kind I am writing in now, small, neat, vellum finish, an ordinary writing pad of the kind one might buy in any shabby little street-corner stationer among the sweeties, perhaps with a wolfhound and round tower on its cover. I probably got it in Dublin before I left, but why I carried it with me through Europe that summer I don't really know; I was never one for writing home, though I probably managed an occasional note, to stave off the anxiety of my elders, who had never travelled outside Ireland except via the emigrant boat, *ollagoaning*, lamenting all the way.

Besides, my wanderings were now accepted in the family with something near fatalism, as a youthful, probably pagan ritual, leading me far from 'mother church, motherland and mother'. I do remember sending a triumphant postcard from Padua to my mother, who had a great devotion to St Anthony, among many other saints of course, and another from Assisi, Giotto's *St Francis Preaching to the Birds*. It was always my casuistical contention that Europe was packed with shrines, where the saints we heard of in church had lived and died, and now the half-century, 1950, had been proclaimed by the Pope himself as a Holy Year, *Anno Santo*, so that I could present myself as a pilgrim, ardent to reach the holy door.

It was also my twenty-first year, and in the absence of any

official recognition of my coming of age, I had planned and was now giving myself a sort of *Wanderjahr*, to assuage the hunger for all sorts of experience which I felt lacking in my native land. It was a rhythm that had become part of my life: I would reach out as far as I could on the Continent, for as long as I could manage, and then return slowly, usually through repatriation, to Ireland. There I would manage to survive, buoyed up by all I had seen and heard, until I had to hit the road again. Years later, such escapes abroad would become part of ordinary Irish student life, but in my urgency I was something of a pioneer, a new kind of Hibernian savage, invading the Continent in search of art and love, *Peregrinus Hibernicus*, a horn-mad celibate with a bright red comb and a roving eye.

It was a different Europe, of course, not criss-crossed with charter planes, not crammed with package tours and student fares. Then you made your way slowly, wearily, by boat and bus and train, waking gradually to some new excitement, like walking out into the aquatic bustle of Venice from Santa Lucia Station. Or cycling through the French countryside, surprised by lines of vines, the thick rustling of maize, giant red tomatoes, a glowing Van Gogh field of *tournesols*. Or the straight line through Paris from the *Gare du Nord* to the Youth Hostel at *Porte d'Orléans*; it made my non-linear intelligence boggle. The fierce roar of the *Autoroute du Sud*, thronged with long-distance lorries and family cars, was still far away, in the crowded future.

I suppose I was planning to keep a Journal; Gide had just received the Nobel Prize and introspection was fashionable. But I did nothing as systematic as that, for now only fragments from that summer float up before me: a curious visit to the head-quarters of the Soviet Zone in Vienna; a night sleeping in a field outside Bologna, waking wet with morning dew; a zealous perusal of the subtleties of Sienese Art, trying to distinguish between all that gold, those slanting eyes! Piecing the jigsaw, I realise that it was a bewildering but necessary summer of growth, a preparation for something unknown, some sensuous epiphany.

The first part takes place in Florence, *Firenze*, where I had dropped off again on my way back from Rome. Yes, I had made it to the Holy City, all the way down the spine of Italy from Venice, my beard now red and ragged, my arms stippled with freckles. And yes, I did visit the four Basilicas, and see the Pope being ferried on the *Sedia Gestatoria*. I was within spitting distance of the pale bespectacled Pacelli, *Pio Dodicesimo*, because I was there as part of an official delegation, the International Conference on Catholic Cinema, to give it its full, sonorous title.

That was because of my work on *The Catholic Eagle* at home in Dublin as a film critic. So I led a double life; nights in the Youth Hostel, a hectic barracks on the outskirts of Rome, where a late bus dropped me off in the evenings; days as a delegate at the Conference, sporting my one suit for official meetings and receptions. A famous Irish actor was attending it also, using the forum as an excuse for a holiday. And he was very friendly to me, bringing me everywhere with him like a mascot, deferring to my unfledged but extreme opinions in literature and art, my wild plans. Together we gaped at the ceiling of the Sistine Chapel, loitered through the endless rooms of the Vatican Gallery. Then back to his central hotel in the evenings, where we had cherries soaked in red wine on the terrace. And if I was lucky he would bring me with him afterwards to a *trattoria*, my one meal of the day. Between the heat and the wine I barely made it back.

But let the journey curve back to Florence, through the white splendour of Rome's new railway station, after the Conference was over, and my generous actor friend had flown away. I had stayed in a pilgrims' hostel on the way down, and been thrown out for returning late; I tried to explain to the priest in charge that I was trying to combine pilgrimage with sightseeing but the philistine refused to see my point. So this time I made my way to the Youth Hostel, another large, thronged, happy building. The night burned with light and voices until well after midnight. And during the day I continued my exploration of Florence, from Ghiberti's Baptistery doors to the Roman theatre at Fiesole, where I sat stunned in the afternoon sunlight.

My problem was time: three days was the limit in any hostel, and though I doubled it by hitchhiking to Siena and back, the time was approaching when I would have to leave. And I had only begun to understand the glory that was Florence! Earnest, intent, insufferable, I was determined to be an apostle of art, a martyr, if necessary, in the cause of beauty; but there seemed no way that I could simply stay on.

I shared the washing up with an English-speaking South African, who was also on his European year before he went home to take over the family business. He was stocky, neat and slow-spoken, but perhaps because we were opposites, we made a good enough team. He knew nothing about art, except that he should know about it, so he probed me for the little I had found out for myself, through a battered copy of an old-fashioned guidebook in my rucksack, which I promised to leave him. There was a Victorian earnestness about Pieter — he probably disapproved of all this paganism but it had to be seen.

So on my last morning he followed me through the city centre for a farewell look, and then bought me a light lunch, a *panino* and glass of wine, in a *trattoria*. We sat in the cool, listening for the rustle of the bead curtain as chatty Italians flowed in and out. All this richness and colour was about to leave my life; my rucksack was stowed under the table and I would shortly be tramping towards the station. I was sullen and down-in-the-mouth, a poor companion.

Sympathetic to my silence, he suggested that I should wait for the night train, and come with him to meet a strange young girl he had found himself beside in a queue at the American Express. 'Very strange,' he emphasised, in his clipped tones, under his little moustache. 'You know how Americans are,' he said, 'very green but very loud. But she did ask me round. God knows what for. Says she's a painter and I told her I'd met this young poet chap from Ireland. Like to know what you'd make of her. Really would.' He sounded uneasy, still terse but tense, for some reason. So instead of the afternoon train to Paris, or hitch-hiking on the dusty fringe of some high road, I found myself squatting on the stone floor of a small studio, at the feet of a young American girl. She was quite young, a little older than me, pretty but shameless by my provincial standards, as she twiddled her brightly painted toes right under our noses. Clearly my South African friend bored her, but she was lonely and wanted to speak English. I had never really known anyone like her, with a halter holding her overflowing breasts, and shorts riding carelessly high on tanned legs. Except that I *had* met her once before....

II

I had met her in the Uffizi Gallery. Since I didn't have enough money to eat at midday, I had taken to staying in a gallery through lunch-time, to avoid the sight of people eating; as well as to increase my knowledge of painting, of course. Trying to stave your hunger by staring at the details of master-works is an interesting exercise in mortification, especially in the heat of the day; what I had developed was a restless and ambulatory form of the siesta, like a mad monk on hunger-strike outside the door of a refectory. Down in the Piazza della Signora, happy tourists were tucking in, under gaily coloured awnings. If I looked that way, my eyes stuck out on stalks, so I stared at the paintings, as if through a magnifying glass.

On bad days, all still lifes were banned. Glorious pyramids of ruddy-cheeked fruit; vermilion cherries; green, black and purple grapes; soft furred peaches: on my imagination's palate they burst endlessly. Streams of juice ran down my chin, seeds stuck to be sucked in my teeth until in the intensity of my hallucination I ran from the room. Sticks of bread doubly disturbed me. Thank God I was in Florence and not in some Dutch museum, with rich rosy sides of beef, freshly hung game or venison, the saliva-raising sight of a Brueghel village feast, full bellies and distended codpieces, rich food and lusty love afterwards. The worst I had to face was Caravaggio's *Adolescent Bacchus*, his face already flushed with the wine fumes, a piled bowl of fruit before him to gorge on.

Sometimes I tried to assuage one hunger by another, spending a long time, for example, in the cool decorum of the Botticelli room. Venus rising from her half shell, a strand of flaxen hair held demurely over her pudenda, her visage pensive; she was as mysterious and refreshing as an early morning by the sea. Luckily, I had not yet become an amateur of the oyster or *coquilles Saint Jacques* or that half shell might have been another source of temptation.

I was especially drawn to the room with the great Titians, large sensuous females at ease in their nudity, as leisurely and complete as domestic animals. The reclining *Venus of Urbino* also had a hand over her gently swelling belly to cover her thatch but the eye slid down that listless, boneless arm to join the fingers; it was a gently inviting slope, not a protective pudic gesture. And her soft, brown eyes and coiled auburn hair seemed to gather one into her rich nakedness, to lie beside her on that tousled linen bedspread where she had drowsed so long, be it only as the pampered lapdog curled beside her crossed calves.

But I would have to avoid even them if I had had no breakfast. The light-headedness of hunger can lead to extreme forms of lust, and sometimes I was less aware of the luminous Venetian tonality of the paintings, less inclined to compare them with Bellini and Giorgione in their use of colour, than overcome by their sulky physical presence. A scraggy frustrated Irish adolescent, I gaped at them hungrily, like the cats thrown in the Coliseum, and sometimes I could hardly hold myself back from leaping through the canvas to bite, even slice, a voluptuous golden haunch. Blake's 'lineaments of gratified desire', I thought, as my stomach growled. Would I ever know such satisfaction?

As I was gazing at them, I realised that someone was watching them and me. It was a young blonde with brown tanned skin and ice-blue eyes, like the corn maiden of some Northern tale. With her cascading hair, her slender but full-breasted figure, she looked as if she had stepped down from the frame of a painting! She had a red belt drawn tightly around her waist and wore bright red slippers of a kind I had seen in the market behind the Duomo. They seemed to flicker back and forth under her light, long skirt, to match her impatience, as she sized me up before speaking: 'Gee, I wish I could lay on the paint like that,' she said in a nasal American voice, almost a whine. 'What's this guy's name again?'

Grateful for the excuse to show off my scant knowledge, I gabbled about Titian, *Tiziano Vecelli*, and his part in the Venetian High Renaissance. She listened with what I hoped was interest, contemplating me with her expressionless eyes. Then she turned on her heel and left with a parting shot that stung: 'Thanks for the lecture, Mick.' She made it sound like *hick*, an insult I knew from my reading. Was it so obvious that I was Irish, a gabbling Paddy? 'I have to run to American Express. See you around sometime, maybe.'

The last word was emphasised, *may-be* drawn out with scorn until it seemed to rhyme with *unlikely* or *not if I see you first, buddy*. So I had bored her. I watched her tight little bum swagger down the corridor away from me, the lift of each hip a gesture of disdain. Or so I thought, looking hopelessly after the first pretty girl I had spoken to in months....

And yet here I was speaking to her again, my head only a short distance from her warm brown legs and knees. And she was finding me amusing, or at least less boring than my South African friend, whom she teased relentlessly. 'Are they really all like you down there? We've got Negroes, too, you know, but you sound like some fruity mixture of British stuck-up and Georgia cracker when you talk about them. Let 'em be, they can't be as bad as you sound. Bet your women like them — they got the old jelly roll.' And she waggled her bottom on the chair, above him.

Pieter did not know how to take her as she rambled on about race and colour and sex — I gathered she was from New York and had definite views about all three. For the moment, I decided to agree with her about them all, if it ensured my being close to her for even a little while longer. Maybe God will be good, I thought with a mixture of faith, hope, and lechery.

Pieter decided to master his irritation by showing that he did not take her seriously; she was too young. 'I think you are just a naughty girl,' he said indulgently, waving at her his imaginary swagger stick, a short ruler he had found on the floor near an easel. She went off into wild giggles.

'Don't you shake your little stick at me, Mr Man,' she said in what I recognised as a parody of a Southern accent. Then when he began to look not only puzzled, but angry: 'Haven't you read Freud, you nuthead? You're wagging that stick at me because you want to beat or fuck me, but you don't dare ask, do you, you silly racist prick?'

Raging, thin-lipped, my South African friend rose to go. He expected me to come with him, but I had been explaining to her earlier about having to leave the Hostel. Watching me hesitate, she saw a chance to hurt him still more.

'Why don't you park your knapsack here? You look too young to be out but you can't be dumber than him. If you are, you can always just sleep on the floor for a few days.'

With a weak attempt at a chilly look, the South African left, and Wandy Lang and I stared at each other. That hot July night in Florence, I slept in her narrow bed, beneath her easel.

III

And spent the rest of the month in that cot, except when we quarrelled and I slept on the stone floor in my sleeping bag. A strange duel took place in that hot narrow cell, on the fourth floor of an old Florentine house: a duel of unequals. There was my timidity, so much a product of my time and place, our forgotten island off the broken coast of Europe, which had largely avoided the War. And her avid American greed for experience, spoilt child of a rich but predatory world. We were both looking for something, but she expected it, I vainly hoped for it; the lately victorious and the colonial victim were bound to be at loggerheads.

She wouldn't help me, at first, during those long, hot nights; every move was left to me. And my knowledge of female anatomy was restricted to picture-gazing: lacking sisters or adventurous girlfriends, I was a typical product of an Irish clerical education, eager but ignorant. Sometimes I made it to the magic centre, but often I fumbled, grappling blindly in that airless tiny oven of a room, where our bodies stuck together like stamps. And every time I fell back, she made sure it hurt.

'I'm not going to help you. You're all that I hate, kids that are clumsy and stupid. Why should I show you the works, you little Irish Catholic prick. Fuck you —'

At first, I tried to give some smart answer, like 'But that's just what I want you to do.' But after tirades like these I usually lay awake; silent, hurt, still hoping. And she would rise in the morning, blithe as if nothing had happened. Then we would go to take a *caffe latte* together, inside the bead curtain if it was too hot, on the sidewalk if there was a cool breeze. And then we would begin our day together, which was usually easier than the night, with her painting, and me trying to write.

And as the days passed, I began to hope against hope that I might be able to please her. She was my meal ticket, of course, and the unsubtle art of freeloading was one I had already learnt a little of in the drab school of Dublin pub life in the late 1940s. But I also believed dimly in my mystic mission as a young poet, and around us lay all the ingredients for an idyll. With that impossible mixture of hunger and idealism, I set out to try and understand this ferocious young woman whom fate had flung directly across my pilgrim path.

Wandy Lang was pretty, rich, but wild and clawing as a lost alley cat. She was not looking for the way out of an Irish Catholic childhood, stumbling towards fulfilment, but seeking something that would anneal, annul the empty ache that was already eating her. Somewhere along the line, someone or something had hurt her, in a more drastic way than all the pious regulations of my education. Or perhaps the combination of money and freedom that her background seemed to offer her was only an illusion that left her still empty and angry. Whatever the reason, she was trying to work it out, in her own strange way, far from her compatriots, in a loneliness that somehow resembled my own intense, Quixotic quest.

Perhaps sex would help? She certainly seemed to have tried it, to judge by her wild language, her ceaseless use of words like prick and ass and cunt. In theory, I was all for calling a spade a bloody shovel, but to hear her pretty young mouth spew swearwords scandalised me; when she was angry it rang like a litany, a litany of desecration, of blasphemy, but also of loss and longing, if I had been able to hear its dark rhythms. But the bruised places in myself had still to unseal themselves, and I could not meet her pain with mine, although it was that hurt which called me to her.

But now her 'thing' was art. Her elder brother was a painter, whom she admired blindly, and wanted to emulate. Although, she emphasised, he would be disgusted if he knew she was daring to paint, herself. He had always discouraged her because he was a real painter, a serious painter, like Paul Klee, or 'Pete' Mondrian, who was the biggest modern painter, who had replaced nature. Did I know his tree series?

I had never heard of Mondrian, and I certainly couldn't judge the kind of painting she was doing, carefully planned with an architecture of lines, constructed with the ruler the South African had waggled at her, and then intently filled-in squares, triangles and lozenges of colour. But she really worked: after breakfast, she set up her easel in the middle of the room to catch what little light came through our high window, and with bare midriff and loosely tied hair, she pointed herself at the canvas silently for hours. Heat flared up the Florentine sky, with its glimpses of red tiled roofs, the ochre façade of a high building. Her hair would tumble sweatily down, her forehead bead, until she unconsciously untied her blouse and stood bare-breasted before the canvas, like a defiant young Amazon. Now that I know more of painter and painting, I know that she was trying to imitate somebody, her brother probably, and his peers, in a pathetic parody of their intent professional preoccupation.

While she sweated before her easel, I tried to write poems. But it was too hot to concentrate properly and I was so obsessed with her presence before me in the small room that I could think only on one subject. Particularly when she stood naked to the waist before the easel, hair rippling down to her hips, oblivious of my surreptitious glances. I tried to write little poems about her, in praise of her unmarked young body, its mixture of sensuousness and childish boldness. They were Chinese lyrics, in the style of Pound, whose incarceration had made him an idol for the Irish young: a prisoner for the cause.

> *Her blonde hair pours*
> *down her studded spine;*
> *bare to the waist,*
> *she stands, my girl.*

Surrounded by the shy lasses of my country, I had touched, but rarely seen breasts. In Ireland, it was the blind leading the blind but with Wandy I could stare and stare endlessly, feasting my eyes on those mysterious forbidden globes before I began to try and net them in words.

> *How warm her white breasts!*
> *Two bowls of cream with*
> *Her nipples, bright cherries.*

Such naïve tenderness! But the ardour of that young man in the Florentine heat reaches out for my indulgence across several decades. We were a pair, a team in our blundering ambition: as she dragged her brush across an area of canvas, or peered before adding a touch of colour, I tried to study her as a painter might, my first life class — but a very modern one, for I was painting a standing nude who was trying to paint an abstract: a nearly Cubist vision of reality!

> *As she works, she pouts.*
> *Her face is young, serious.*
> *Her eyes sharp blue.*

And so forth. One day she looked over my shoulder. 'Hey there,' she exclaimed, 'you make me sound nice.' And she looked at me with warm, surprised eyes. Then she leaned over and gave me a quick kiss, the first she had ever given me in daylight.

From then on, the notebook followed us everywhere, to museums, restaurants, cafés, sometimes churches. She had taken to drawing in it; wild, impulsive scrawls to go with the poems. Clearly, I had found the way to her heart, for even in bed she began to ease up, relaxing her guard to the point where she seemed almost tender. And I was beginning to improve a little, learning how to please, to be a lover, although she was already so precocious that I lagged far behind, a blundering innocent, who had even to be taught how to kiss properly. She taught me other tricks, things that I only half understood, bending her urgent young body like a bow, as she searched avidly for the next sensation; arching her spine, like a cat, in shudders of self-delight.

Somehow, desperately, I felt that this was wrong, that wild experiment should be the joyous fruit of love, not its budding point. But who was I to argue with her? She already knew so much more than I did about the mechanics of sex that our couplings were bound to seem clumsy and ludicrous, forcing her into the incongruous role of the older woman, the instructress of male naïveté. 'No, touch me here. Higher up. And keep that other hand down. And slowly, gently. Women like to be stroked.' Or, in another mood: 'Don't tell me you never did it like this! That's the best way to penetrate, to get it deep. Look at the animals; I thought you said you were brought up on a farm. Some cowboy you are!' And when I was spent, her hand or tongue would reach out, to revive me, rise me.

I did my best, or thought I did, to follow her urgent instructions. And she tried to control, restrain whatever irritation my incompetence caused her, compared to her previous male friends. Whoever had taught her the erotic arts had done it well, for there seemed to be little that she did not know: taking baths together like mad children, moving the bed until it was under the wall mirror, dancing together naked before we slid to the floor or bed. And for a while we seemed to enter into, at least hover near, the sweet conspiracy of lovers, although such words of endearment were not part of her harsh vocabulary. The widow next door, for instance, was shocked to discover that there was a young man staying with Wandy, a half-naked savage with red hair. Since we shared a lavatory on the landing it was difficult to avoid meeting, but she would lower her eyes when she saw us passing. And once when Wandy came to the door to kiss me, forgetting to cover her breasts, rather not bothering, the dark, startled Italian woman crossed herself several times, lifting the crucifix on her dark dress.

IV

To be twenty-one, to have a girlfriend — a mistress! — and to have the run of Florence; it seemed like the fulfilment of the dream that had lured me all the way from Ireland. I had padded down its narrow streets for more than a week before I met her and now she had given me a month's reprieve, with the added pleasure of being a guide to a beautiful young woman. For she seemed to have lived in Florence as if it were any flat American city, seeing, sensing its quality without understanding it. She knew it was a place to be, but why wasn't clear to her. So the little I knew I lavished on her while I kept boning up in the British Institute library, to impress her, as I had tried that first time in the Uffizi. Laying my small treasures of knowledge before her like a faithful spaniel, I was often oblivious to the ironies of the situation, as when I introduced her to the Fra Angelicos in the Convent of San Marco.

The first time we got turned away because of the shorts and halter she was wearing. But we came back and in those cool cloisters shaded by flowerbeds and Lebanese cedars, we saw the fruits of the saintly painter's meditation, a guide to prayer, a fervent hymn to the glory of a Christian God. A long-fingered *St Dominic* clasping, embracing the Cross down which ran the ruby rivulets of Christ's passion, the delicate dialogue of the *Annunciation*, the blue of the Virgin's cloak and the multicoloured wings of the angel Gabriel, the rainbow-tinted dance of the Elect in his *Last Judgement*; I could not help but hush before such feeling. These were not the gaudy repository images of my Ulster Catholic childhood — they seemed to breathe a mystical aroma, as light and radiant as the wing of a butterfly. Somewhere in me my fading belief stirred, the very faith I felt I had to disdain in order to live.

But for Wandy they were only pretty gewgaws, relics from a world long dead, inspired by emotions that no one would ever need again. Emerging from that rich silence she enquired plaintively: 'They're pretty colours, but why did he have to waste so much time painting virgins and saints and old stuff like that? We've left all that behind now. My brother says real painting should only be about itself.'

So I brought her to the Medici Palace, also built by Michelozzo. For me it was a Poundian paradigm of creative order, the walls where the Medici, those munificent Mafia, lived and lavished their wealth. They were all there in the ornate frescoes of Gozzoli, Emperors and Patriarchs invited from the East to join them in a stately procession through the landscape of Tuscany. It might be based on the Magi, but the emphasis was on earthly glory, clothes stiff with ornament, gloriously caparisoned horses. She looked for a long time at a handsome young man, astride a leopard.

'I like him,' she said, and when I explained that he was the brother of Lorenzo the Magnificent, she added: 'He's as pretty as my brother,' and smacked her lips.

She went silent at last in the Medici crypt before the unfinished torsos of Michelangelo. She lingered before *Dusk* and *Dawn,* froze like a gun dog before *Day*, fighting to free himself, large-muscled and intent, from cloudy matter. But it was the graceful, sombre figure of *Night*, its large breasts and bent head, with sad, brooding eyelids, which finally got to her. 'Jee-sus,' she exclaimed, 'I thought you said these were done by a man. He must have been pretty lonely to feel like that. I didn't know you could get that deep down chipping a stone. It's as bad as the blues.'

She tried to thank me, in her own way, for trying to show her so much, for sharing. Day after day passed without a dispute, and in bed at night she was, if not submissive, more subdued in her demands, less insulting in her remarks on my performance. Something akin to peace began to grow between us. Surprised by beauty daily, we made our fumbling efforts to create it ourselves, and afterwards we strolled by the Arno, holding hands as the sun lit the red of the roofs, the intense yellow-brown of the river.

On every walk we seemed to discover something, a lovely *Venus* in the Boboli Gardens, *The Deposition of Christ from the Cross* by Pontormo, in a church near the Ponte Vecchio. And if I didn't know about Mondrian, I had heard of Masaccio, Big Tom, and led her to obscure churches where the walls were covered with his work — Adam and Eve fleeing from paradise, his head bowed, her hands shading her body from a relentless red angel. This time she did not complain about but admired the treatment of the subject; after all, Florentine painting was a disciplined art, with the kind of geometry of perspective that she was looking for in Modern Art: colour called to colour, shape balanced shape.

From the blue and white cherubs of della Robbia to the flower-covered meadows of Botticelli's *Primavera*, I tried to offer it all to her, watching as she watched, ignorant but excited, a child gazing at a galaxy of dazzling stars. Back in the Botticelli room she danced for joy, like the three Graces in their transparent veils, and when I told her that Venus rising from her shell was Simonetta, the beloved of the young man riding the Gozzoli leopard, she clapped her hands like someone listening to a nursery story for the first time. Especially when I added: 'She makes me think a bit of you, when you look thoughtful, with your hair down.' And danced for me again, shyly moving her lissom body to the inaudible rhythms of the paintings. My heart was in my mouth as I watched, her graceful heel and instep echoing the flaxen-haired Florentine beauties of the wall. And then she bowed, and broke into a phrase of Italian I did not know: '*Mi piace molto ballare,*' I really love to dance.

When she had first come to Florence she had tried to learn Italian from a family to which she had an introduction, again arranged by her brother. Now she asked them if she could bring me along and told them proudly that I was a poet. With the deference of older Europeans to any mention of high art, I was received, scraggy, sweating in my single suit, as if I were the real thing, instead of a gaping novice.

Red wine flowed, *pastasciutta* and liquid syllables of Italian that sounded splendid even if I only dimly understood. And when our host began to quote Dante, with all the sonorous intimacy of a Florentine, I responded with Yeats, boom answering boom, like church bells ringing across the city. For the first time I heard those great lines describing the plight of the doomed lovers, Paolo and Francesca, their adulterous eyes meeting over a beloved book:

> *When we read how a lover slaked his drouth*
> *upon those long desired lips, then he*
> *who never shall be taken from my side*
>
> *all trembling, kissed my ardent mouth.*

and I countered with:

> *Beloved, may your sleep be sound*
> *That have found it where you fed.*

Our host's wife beamed. Wandy beamed. And when they wouldn't let us leave after lunch but ushered us for the siesta into a small white room with a real bed with laundered linen sheets, Wandy was beside herself with girlish delight. 'They must think we're married or engaged or something.' And she blushed. And in those cool white sheets we made love with no preconceptions, no inhibitions, sweetly, tenderly, turning to each other with muted cries of delight, nibbling and hugging like children before we started again, our lips still joined by a light skein of kisses. That afternoon was her richest gift to me, a glimpse of near ecstasy, of the sensuous fulfilment I longed for in my damp, distant island. And like all such moments it had a scent of permanence, a small addition to the sum of sweetness in the world. Finally she fell asleep, her blonde head resting on my numbed arm, in total ease.

> *In the crook of my arm*
> *my love's head rests;*
> *in each breath*
> *I taste her trust.*

V

That was our high point, the crest of the wave. But it couldn't last, it seems; we soon plunged down. Already that evening, as we stumbled home, she had begun to turn sour. Between the harmony of the afternoon and the airless heat of her little room, the dinginess of the narrow iron bed, was a distance she couldn't, wouldn't cross. When she was in that mood she had to yield to every caprice, however hurtful. There is a certain kind of character that needs to strike out, to wound, and if the victim cares enough to complain, all the worse for them. I fought back at first, but when I found that not only was it useless but it made things much worse, I lapsed into stricken silence.

As she did also, except that she could dredge depths of melancholy, of sadness, that I had never seen in anyone before. As the heat grew daily, we took to going to a suburban swimming pool, to escape from the baking claustrophobia of her little studio. The pool was a gaudy, massive imitation of a Roman Baths, the kind of official architecture that flourished during the Mussolini period. Like most young Americans, Wandy Lang could swim like a fish, used to pools and swimming coaches from her infancy. And like most young Irishmen, I had not been properly taught, and floundered nervously at the shallow end, despising my own pale freckled skin.

And for most young Italians, the Baths was a theatre in which to strut, and show off their wares. They wore crotch-tight swimming trunks and as they looked at her they stroked themselves, openly. And she seemed to like it, to welcome it; there were very few other women present and she had their full attention, especially as she wore the first two-piece I had ever seen, exposing her acorn-brown navel, that cup from which I had newly learnt to drink. When she struck into the water they dipped and dived around her, like dolphins. And when she stretched down to cool, they paraded like distended fighting cocks; one could nearly smell the sperm. As I climbed gingerly in at the shallow end, to practise the breast stroke, they raced past, showering me with spray.

Humiliated, I sat with a towel around my burnt shoulders and tried to contemplate the water, as a kind of exercise. Water in swimming pools changes appearance more than in any other container. In a pool, water is controlled and its rhythms reflect not only the sky but, because of its transparency, the depth of the water as well. If the surface is almost still and there is a strong sun, a dancing line with all the colours of the spectrum will appear anywhere. I tried to share the intensity of my contemplation with Wandy, appealing to her pictorial sense, but she only grunted, as if I were a boring schoolboy, distracting her from the company of grown-ups. My appeal to our artistic comradeship was in vain.

One afternoon I could take no more, and tried to protest to Wandy, where she lay on the edge of the pool, holding her shoulders and breasts up to the sun, then untying her bikini halter to turn her breasts downwards. This move always delighted her audience, especially since she did it slowly, to let them feast their eyes on her body. I could neither stand nor understand it: I had begun to love that body, and that she should let them gape and slaver over it was beyond me.

'Shut up, you little puritan,' she snapped back at me. 'Just because you can't swim properly you want everyone else to go round hunched up like a cripple. You Irish hate water and sun.' I tried to explain to her that, despite their preening and pushing, her admirers were as frustrated as any Irish provincial. The dark cloud of *la mamma*, as well as holy Mother Church, hung over the home; she was dealing with, teasing, regaling the most conventional males in Europe, with a double set of values — one for their own women, the other for whores and foreigners. Their only experience of sex, outside marriage, would be through the brothel, and there, money ruled, especially since the dollars of the American army of occupation had ruined the trade. They were full of contempt for foreigners, especially women, on whom they would exact revenge for their humiliation in war. If she did let them near her, they would only despise and drop her.

I was brilliant, I thought, a week's bile exploding in a sermon that surprised even myself. Had the fury of Savonarola, as well as Fra Angelico, infected me after San Marco, where I had returned to visit his tiny cell and contemplate on my own? Certainly there was a stench of burning flesh in my speech, a furious rhetoric which wrapped up both her and them, my disappointment at her desertion, my jealousy of their sun-warmed maleness. But most of the information was not mine; I had collected it, unconsciously, from film after film, where the tension between the sexes in Italy inflamed the celluloid.

'So you think you know it all,' she said angrily, after we came plodding home from the pool, and began to pull off our heat-dampened clothes. She was sitting on the bed, half naked, her skirt already shed to the floor, showing her warm gold thatch. 'Well, I've been fucking since I was fifteen.'

Silence.

'And when did *you* start?' She answered herself easily. 'You never did, did you? Boy, your country must be backward. You hardly even know where the cunt is. Well, take a good look at it now — for the last time.' And she lay back, provocatively spread-eagled on the bed, the pretty red shape of her sex, part wound, part flower, held open to me. But when I came forward to touch her, she jack-knifed up, laughing and jeering. 'You're not going to use me for your anatomy lesson, brother. If they didn't teach you anything about sex in your country, don't come crying to me. And don't try to tell me about men; I know. You're ashamed of your body, you can't talk. Before I met you, you didn't even know how to clean your foreskin, a real hillbilly. Christ, I don't know what they did to you in your silly schools, but your prick isn't part of you —'

She was right, of course; in school we wore shorts in the showers when we came to hose ourselves down after another sweaty, exhausting game of football, which seemed designed to drain us. And yearly we got a lecture on sex from a priest, his face brick red with embarrassment as he tried to explain something that he barely knew about himself. Our information was garnered furtively, in dirty jokes and stories. Meanwhile the sap rose urgently, blindly, in our bodies, adolescents in the charge of celibates who were more scared than us of that pulsing power, the fermenting energy of sex that could not be denied, or channelled for long. But why did she have to mock me? Was I not more to be pitied than laughed at, to use our local Ulster expression? Between her early excess of knowledge and my ignorance was a gap that only goodwill could cross, and Wandy did not see why she should take charge of my re-education, any more than I was willing to accept her coarseness. Who had initiated her into sex, leaving her with such a mixture of avidity and terrible loneliness?

Meanwhile, we quarrelled, heat, anger, frustration crackling through that narrow room. After each attack, she tried to make it up to me, pleading silently, almost childishly for forgiveness, in little ways that tore my heart. She would bring me a newspaper, for example, or an expensive book from one of the international bookshops. Or a brightly coloured pencil with a rubber on the top; a new fountain pen. But I wouldn't come to the pool again, determined not to be hurt by her, or those grinning young Italian males, shorts bulging like nets after a day's catch. I had had enough machismo to last me for a lifetime; instead I trudged to the cool of the British Institute library, absorbing myself again in books, trying to blot out the images of longing and rage that surged in me. It was another version of my artistic hunger-strike and about as successful: a sex-starved bookworm, I could not, like the common or garden worm, split in two and have sex with my other half.

Suddenly a detail from Berenson's *Florentine Painters of the Renaissance* would come alive, and a slender, delicious young body would stand, not before me, but before a gaping crowd who devoured her with their eyes. Then I fled to poetry, laboriously trying to decipher the message of the *Duino Elegies*. But then Rilke would betray me, his spiritual search turned sensuous, and I would nearly weep with jealousy and desire, the words fading on the page before me. Where could I be safe from the fragrant, furious presence of that wild young woman whom I both adored and loathed? A raw little American bitch who could scarcely read — how had I allowed her to shred me apart like this when, a star student, I already knew so much more about everything than she did? Except sex; the sharp perfume of her young, hot body rose in my nostrils, until like a maddened monk plagued by noonday visions of lewdness, I nearly swooned. I was in love with this terrible young woman, in love, maybe, with the idea that I had been sent to help her. But how? I struggled for some formula of acceptance, suitable for an Ulster ascetic, an Armagh anchorite.

When I wouldn't return to the pool, she organised a trip to the real sea, to Viareggio, perhaps because I said Rilke had once stayed there. And how sweetly careful her preparations were! She had a picnic basket, with a whole cooked chicken, a flask of wine, a good cheese and ripe fruit; just like any normal sweetheart, wife or mother, organising an outing with a loved one. We bathed, and lay under a parasol, and bathed again, running with linked hands into the waves. And to dance along the strand, that private intense dance of pleasure which I had not seen for a long time.

> *By the seashore*
> *my love dances:*
> *the waves press*
> *to kiss her feet.*
>
> *Phoebus Apollo,*
> *the sun god,*
> *the light bringer,*
> *has blessed our feast.*

But before we were bouncing back to Florence again by bus, her mood had already swung back to bitterness. There was a song she kept speaking of, a song of Billie Holiday; a name, like Mondrian, which I had never heard of in Ireland. It was

'Gloomy Sunday', and it was what she called blues, based on an old Hungarian tune, adapted by the doomed black singer. It had caused so many deaths, she said, that it was sometimes known as the Hungarian Suicide Song, and it was banned by some radio stations for its melancholy. If you listened carefully, you would realise that it was the lament of someone deep into drugs, for whom life was too much pain to sustain. And she told me of Lady's life, the heavy drugs, the brutal lovers; a Black boyfriend claimed to have met her.

At this point, the seemingly endless cloud of our quarrels induced a kind of hallucinatory confusion. Did she possess some kind of radio or record player, an early portable phonograph? She certainly crooned the words to herself every evening in the hot darkness, as the light faded in the small, high window. I watched as the head I had tried to love sank lower and lower, drowning in a sadness, a thick, black gloom that resounded through those strange, husky tones, like the dark wax wasps exude:

> *Sunday is gloomy*
> *My hours are slumberless.*
> *Dearest, the shadows*
> *I live with are numberless....*

Lulled by the spell of the song, she would topple slowly sideways to the floor, asleep. Above her was the easel she no longer used much; the few half-hearted attempts she had made recently reminded me of a pump or bucket trying to dredge from a long-dried well. Something was terribly wrong, and I didn't know what to do about it. I was as unequipped as I had been at the pool to sound the depths to which she was sinking, to revive and rescue her.

> *In the window*
> *daylight fails.*
> *My love's head*
> *also falls....*

The ochre shade
of the walls
fades; cracks
on a grey rock.

Love once
lit the room,
is there any
way back?

VI

Towards the end of the month, her money began to run out. What were we to do? Half-heartedly, I offered to change my last traveller's cheque from Cook's, the one that was supposed to bring me to Paris. She shook my offer away, partly because she understood my reluctance only too well, and also because, perhaps, she wanted us to maintain our roles. It had to be her money, her flat, if she was to keep the upper hand in our relationship — to call the shots, as she coarsely said. 'I'm not going to raid the poorbox' was another mocking reply, when I tried again.

So I waited, using all my newly won training in restraint. After a day or so sucking oranges, propping her head with her fist in total, sulky silence, her features distorted, she seemed to come to some decision. She told me curtly to stick around, while she went to see the owner of the flat. She came back with him, and another, to my eyes, ancient Italian lizard, whom I had already seen in the Black Market when we went to change dollars. A typical *sensale*, behind his old-fashioned linen suit.

We sat talking for a while in pidgin English and then suddenly I felt as if there was a vacuum in the room. No one bothered to speak, all politeness was dropped as they stared at me, or rather right through me. Thick as a root, I finally still got the message. I went out and wandered the endless streets, raging. Even Florence couldn't please me: the statue of David seemed brazen, brutal, like the smirks of the young Italians on their farting motorcycles and lambrettas. At least I had a girl and didn't have to go to whores, as they did, or pester foreigners in the streets. Finally I decided to turn back: why had she driven me out for those repulsive old codgers, with their triumphant leers, like Rembrandt's *Susanna and the Elders*? Surely she would not let them touch her young beauty? I felt as protective as Galahad, as wrathful as Savonarola.

She was cleaning up the place when I got back. She had borrowed a broom from our surprised neighbour, and was wielding it well, with all our clothes, belongings, tidied into a corner, and the only carpet hanging through the small window. I came in slowly, spotted that my rucksack was still on its peg, and sat on the bed to be out of her way. It had been made, which was not usual, with the sheet tucked under the pillow.

'What happened?' I stammered finally, when she slowed down. She did not answer so I waited until she sat down again, on the only place she could, on the bed next to me.

'What h-h-happened?' I tried again. 'I ought to know. I-I want to know what they did.'

She turned her face towards me, blank at first, that deliberate blankness I had come to know so well, which baffled and troubled me. Then a rising anger sharpened her features, made her blue eyes blaze.

'So you want to know, Mr Irishman, Mr James Joyce the Second, the budding poet. A little unwashed priestly prick is more like it. Well, you can hear my confession, you pious little bastard. They wanted to fuck me, the old farts, but they'd be too afraid, too afraid of heart attacks, too afraid of mama. So they just felt me up —'

Dumb, head down, angry at her, sad for her, ashamed of myself, I listened. There was no escape from, no recourse for, what I was hearing.

'Yeah, they felt me up, good and plenty. One stuck his fingers up, while the other mauled my breasts. Then they changed around, like a ball game. You're shocked, aren't you, little Mr Know-It-All from Nowheresville? Maybe I even liked it better than your fumbling. My nipples hardened, anyway.'

The anger was subsiding in her voice; that strange sadness again.

'The owner spotted that of course, and the bastard stopped. He said I was a bad girl and should be punished.'

At last I was indignant. 'Surely, you didn't let them?'

'Did I what? We needed the money, didn't we?' She turned to face me, on the bed.

'Yeah, I let them spank me a bit and tickle me with the ruler but the bruises won't show. And now we don't need to worry about the rent. And look under that pillow: we'll be able to eat out tonight.'

And so we did, splendidly, under a trellis lit with tiny coloured lanterns. We had melon and *prosciutto*, *bistecca alla fiorentina*, and pints of Chianti. As we made our way back she staggered; she had been talking volubly about her family, how her father didn't love her mother any more, and had been fucking around, of her admiration for her brother, 'who is going to be a great painter, you'll see', but was probably bent.

'But he has the prettiest boyfriends,' she said. 'I wish he'd pass them on to me. I wouldn't even mind climbing in with them: I love my brother, damn it. I hope he doesn't kill himself.'

As she cried out the last sentence people turned to look after us in the street. At first she didn't notice, launched into her monologue. 'But they don't want the kid sister. Only the old geezers come sniffing after me. Especially in Europe — everyone's so mixed-up over here.'

And then she saw the shock and amusement of the passers-by, who skirted us, as I propped her along: a drunken young girl was not a normal sight in Italy.

'Fucking Italians,' she screamed, turning to give them the finger. 'Why don't you go and get laid at home, you greaseballs. You fawning fuckers.'

There were two theatrically dressed *carabinieri* at the end of the street, and I didn't want them to spot her. I had already some experience of the hatred Italian police could show for visitors who got out of hand; in every hostel there was someone who had a grim story. Besides, at long last here was a situation I was familiar with. I held her up as straight as I could, hauled her up the stairs, and when she lurched towards the bed I helped her to undress, the now-crumpled skirt and stockings she wore for special outings, to get into churches and restaurants, posing briefly as a modest American miss.

Slack and vulnerable she lay across the bed, drunken mirth slowly breaking down into something even deeper than her usual sadness. Desperation, perhaps?

'They'll be back, of course, the greasy bastards, old meat-balls. They know what I am, they know they can do anything with me. For them I'm just a little American whore. And maybe they're right. Anything goes —' She began to cry, a shallow stream that made her features ugly, nearly old. 'But you don't know who I am. And you never will.' And again she crooned:

> *Sunday is gloom–y*
> *with shadows I spend it all.*
> *My heart and I*
> *have decided to end it all.*

That night I tried to hold her gently, to console her, but she kept pushing my hands away, as if I were molesting her. 'Go away, go away,' she cried, from the depths of her offended youth. 'Leave my tits alone, they're mine, damn you, they're mine.' As she turned and moaned in the hot night, I lay awake beside her. I was at sea, out of my depth completely. I liked what I could understand of her, the childish eagerness when she saw something beautiful, clapping her hands before a Botticelli, doing her little dance when something I had written pleased

her. But her other side frightened me. What she called my
awkward body pulsed with need, and yes, I was ashamed of it, as
I had been taught to be, in the gloomy corridors of school.
'Take your hands out of your pockets, boys!' rang out the
Dean's reprimand. Or in the intimate dark of the confessional:
'Don't defile your body, the temple of the Holy Ghost.' But I
was anxious to get rid of that shame, to be free. Until I was, I
couldn't help her, and I was beginning to be afraid of her
games, those emotional snakes and ladders that exhausted me.

That evening she had taken our notebook and scrawled furiously in it; what had she drawn? As she snored slightly into
dawn, eyes and hair matted with tears and sweat, and the air
cooled a little, I looked at the last pages. There was a scrawl of
bodies, pricks and cunts coarsely entangled, in a blind ritual of
defilement. She had given the sequence of squirming bodies a
title which I could just make out: SEX IS SHIT.

VII

Next morning, I made my ultimate throw. Insular and ignorant I
might be, but things were adding up even in my dim mind. And
I was desperate for her goodwill. I went with my passport and
last traveller's cheque to a bank and when she woke up (came to
was more like it, rubbing blears from swollen eyes), a warm
breakfast, *caffe latte* and fresh bread, was waiting.

She munched in silence and I let her be, knowing a little
about the dull throb of a hangover. As she brushed the crumbs
away, I ran the dishes under the sink, and then came over to
stand by the bedside. She looked at me with a new, strange
expression, a blend of pleading hangdog and weary defiance. I
knelt by the bedside and took her lovely head in my hands. She
began to weep again.

I slid in beside her, and parting the long matted coils of her
hair, rocked her like a child, my hands around her shoulders.
She still did not speak, and with slow hunger, my hands moved

down towards the warm mounds of her breasts. As I grasped them, her tears began to flow down, thick and fast. As she cried and cried, I grew wilder, pinching the rising spikes of her nipples, drinking her tears like a lapdog. Then I drove my tongue into her mouth, tasting the coppery tang of stale wine.

At long last, the tables were turned. So often that month she had taunted and tormented me, for my awkwardness, for my smell even. 'You stink like a dog,' she would say, wrinkling her nose in mock disgust. 'Don't Irish men know how to wash their groins?' Now, broken and uncertain, she lay at my mercy, accepting if not returning my hectic, blind advances as I forged and foraged my way. Most of what I did she had taught me herself, reluctantly; instead of the slow lingering lip kisses of Hollywood, the probing language of the tongue, moving from one orifice to another, the mouth, the navel, the soft nest of the quim.

At times during my apprenticeship she had frightened me with her intensity, reaching out for me again and again, where I lay weary and empty: 'Come on, little worm.' And when she had ruthlessly drained me, she thrust my head down between her thighs, rubbing my face against her warm, moist fur until I choked. Now I licked and drove like a madman, my whole body in a fury of sensual release; emotional revenge. She might not like it, but her body did, as whimpering she came, with harsh cries almost like pain, her body spread-eagled like a starfish, underneath mine. But I still held my fire, hoarded my spunk, waiting by instinct for some last ritual of violation. She was so wide open now that I slid in and out of her, with a wet smack like a second kiss.

I stopped at one point, to find her eyes watching me, not bold any more, but the eyes of a frightened young girl, pleading for release, and I felt like a hunter, hovering near his prey. But I was still not satisfied: a mad energy of resentment burned in me, as though I were waging war against some ghostly antagonist who stood between us, that someone who had first discovered and used this body for his own purposes. Move by move, I was tracking him down, perhaps even becoming him, in order to displace, drive him away for ever; destroy him, if necessary.

Suddenly I flipped her over, and parted her legs. I mounted her, as she had taught me; she raised her buttocks obediently, a small hand reaching back to press my hangings. But instead of the usual entrance, her rosy cleft, I probed, then sank, like a bayonet, into the fold of her arse. Deep in her fundament I finally relaxed, and the seed poured. She cried out.

We lay side by side, in silence, afterwards. 'Is that what your brother did to you?' I asked at last.

She nodded, through tears.

'Then tell me about it,' I commanded.

VIII

As she talked, I saw a large house somewhere in the country, outside New York, perhaps Long Island or Connecticut, the kind of comfortable barn I had seen in so many films. Her father was away, most of the time, working on Wall Street; he took the commuter train from a nearby station, most mornings, and returned at cocktail time. It was the rhythm of her childhood, Mother fixing a pitcher of martinis before going to fetch Daddy at the station, when he had not rung to say that he was staying overnight in New York. It seemed a conventional picture, strange to me only in its assumption of continually replenished riches.

Then, in her early teens, her parents had begun to quarrel. She would waken to the sound of raised, angry voices, broken glass, and later, blows and cries. She knew her elder brother would be awake too, lying and listening, so one night, when she was tired crying alone, she tippytoed down to his room. He always slept naked and it was comforting to snuggle against his warm length, leaner but larger than her teddy-bear. She came back the next night again, and they lay huddled together, listening to the warring voices below; clinging to each other like babes in the wood, as the tall trees lashed and roared.

Absorbed in their deadly fight, their parents noticed nothing. Then one night, something happened; as she lay in her brother's arms, secure and warm from the frightening sounds, that senseless screeching, she felt his groin grow large and warm against hers. Silently, in the darkness, he began to move into her. She had played naughty games with high-school boys, her mouth sore from kisses, her neck and arms covered with love-bites. But this was in a different league: her brother was seven years older than her, and already a young adult, who had made his own sexual choices, sought his own world of escape.

Although he loved his sister, and tried to defend his mother, he had little or no sexual interest in women, was, indeed, already a practising homosexual. So while he showed her how it was done, and let her handle him, he did not care to satisfy the wild cravings he aroused, took pleasure, maybe, in thwarting them, preoccupied with his own revenges. Whatever he might do for her, it had to end with her sucking him or accepting to be buggered. It was what happened with his boyfriends, of course, but he also told her that it would keep her from getting pregnant.

For three years they had gone on like that, until their parents were separated, and the house was sold. By then she was eighteen, and although she dated boys at college, she found them too naïve to understand her needs; their pawings seemed grotesque. Her relationship with her brother still held her, a guilty secret, and she would slip away to see him, as often as she could. She loved him completely but when she stayed overnight in his studio loft in lower Manhattan, he would rarely sleep with her, although he was still glad to see her. Instead, he used her as bait to attract older men from Uptown, gallery owners, dealers and the like. He was determined to make a name for himself as a painter, and she was glad to be able to serve him, for she admired him completely; he was her lord and master. So sleeping with other men who could help him was a bit like sleeping with him; she would tell them about him and his work, sometimes pass them along, if he fancied them, as he did one marvellous black jazz musician. She would do anything for him as long as he would let her stay by his side. Their father paid for Art School and the rent of the loft but her brother hated him: he blamed him for the break-up and for their mother's unhappiness and looked forward to when he could move away, make it on his own.

And he had, with a good first show, and a contract afterwards. But then something horrible had happened; usually his boyfriends had liked her, treated her like a mascot, and let her hang around, being helpful. It made a pathetic little scene, a young girl, sitting studiously beside her brother as he painted, waiting for him to throw a word her way, a stray among the fairies. There was a little blonde boy from Cleveland, Ohio, however, who only pretended to be her friend, and schemed to get rid of her, tittle-tattling about things she had said and done. And when he moved in to live with her brother, she was not allowed to stay over at the flat, and even her visits became uncomfortable. He no longer needed her. One night he told her angrily that he didn't want to think about 'all that mess' any more — he had his own life.

Neither did she, after such pain, but she couldn't find a way back to where she should be. So she asked her father to send her to Europe; she didn't know how much he suspected about her goings on but he had agreed, without conditions. He was worried about her not dating any more and hanging around so much with his pervert son. She didn't think he was as bad as her brother thought; he had a younger woman, and seemed quite contented. All he asked was a postcard now and then, and she had his number if anything happened to her.

But Europe hadn't worked. Everything and everybody seemed so poor, so desperate; many of them didn't wash properly, and there were no showers, or even proper baths. The little hotel she had stayed at in London had only one bath and you had to pay extra to use it; when all the machinery got working, it was like a steam engine. And English girls had dirt under their painted fingernails and didn't know how to lay on make-up properly; they applied it on what was left of yesterday's. And those funny Turkish toilets in France where you had to squat: it was kinda funny but after a while you felt hemmed in. And she never seemed to meet anyone young, though men followed her around everywhere, especially in Paris and Italy. As she blathered on about the shortcomings of the countries I had just been travelling through, so excitedly, I kept pressing her for more details, for more clues.

Yes, she had had a few affairs, one with a rich creep in Milan — 'what else is there to do in that city, you can't eat the Last Supper every night!' — another with a young sailor in Sicily. 'He was so good-looking, and knew how to move his body like a black boy does' — that made me squirm — 'but, boy, he was boring. He wanted to come back with me to America. Imagine bringing him home to mother. He thought I was the girl equivalent of a GI meal ticket.' But in the end there was something about sex with men that had begun to disgust her: all that rooting around. I remembered the Irish street-corner description of sex — *getting your hole*.

She had been picked up by an older woman when she was in Rome and had spent some good weeks with her. There was something new and different about sleeping with a woman: they understood better what it was like to be a sexual victim, used and abused. And a woman understood another woman's body, whereas men were obsessed by their silly pricks, up and down, in and out. A skilful tongue could do just as much.

So much for *mise*, Mr Meself, Ireland's gift to womanhood, and future star of art and love. Whether she was at long last being honest or determined to get her own back, after what I had just done, or a mixture of both, was beyond me. I had travelled farther and faster in a single month than in many years of my previous existence, trying to keep up with this sexual meteor. From cunnilingus to incest and lesbian love; if I had been looking for experience it had washed over me, nearly swamped me. We looked at each other warily, in silence. She had stopped crying.

IX

We didn't last long after that. An unfinished painting stood on the easel, with a dirty towel thrown over it. And I didn't try to make love to her any more — to *bang*, as she now crudely called it in our rare conversations. Even the weather had become murky with freakish storms that lit up our little window, high as in a prison cell. More often than not, I lay on the floor, coming awake to harsh flashes of lightning.

And the walls of that small stone-flagged room were beginning to feel like a prison, a narrow airless place from which I might never escape. In the end, I could take no more. Such brutal rhythms of aggression and affection were beyond me: I wanted love, yes, or at least mutual desire, but not humiliation again. I tried to explain what I felt to Wandy but she was lost in her strange torpor, a kind of pleasureless self-regard which a little Irish *schmuck* (another word she taught me) could not understand.

Neither of us talked much, neither of us wrote in the notebook. So I resolved to leave as I had originally planned. True to form, I borrowed money from her to pay for the train to Paris, although I saved part of it by hiding myself in the lavatory after the frontier, squatting determinedly while people pushed at the door. *Je suis malade, laissez-moi*. And I was.

We had a last meal, in our favourite neighbourhood restaurant. Obscurely honouring the occasion, I wore my only suit again, tie and drip-dry nylon shirt. We still didn't speak much, although it was good, especially the straw-covered bottle of Orvieto. 'Would you like another?' she asked timidly. 'I find it sometimes helps to be a little drunk on trains.' And she tried to smile, that wan aftertaste of shame and gentleness which had sometimes won me back.

Impressing myself at any rate, I did not accept. Instead, we had two *grappas*, those fiery liqueurs that stir the most sluggish tongue. It was our last hour together: she in her light-coloured skirt, high heels and silk stockings; I in my brown suit, almost like adults after what was, for me, at least, my first almost love affair. There was a girl awaiting my return to Ireland, but if I had failed in Florence, surrounded by warmth and beauty, would I not fail again in the dripping, claustrophobic melancholy of Dublin?

Perhaps sensing my mood, she made her last play. 'Look,' she said, 'it wasn't all that bad. I know I was tough on you but I can't help it: I'm not used to having a friend, a boy nearly my own age. I thought you just wanted to fuck me like all the others. And then drop me if the dollars dried up. Maybe you did too, a bit, but you did try to talk to me, and most of them don't. You're really the kind of pal I need, someone I can trust when I get so goddamn lonely. Maybe I could still find the way back, with your help. I was stupid and mean when I said you were awkward. You're really sensitive and sweet, a nice guy, if I'd given you more of a chance. I promise I won't spike you again, if you stay. I'll let you love me up, all you want, if you can just wait —'

It was, for her, a long speech. And I hesitated, for they were words I had longed to hear for some time. But now I didn't trust them, or myself, any more; the protective valves of the heart had closed, I had sealed myself away from her. Was it only selfishness and was I leaving her to drown? In Paris, the tribes were beginning to gather: Dónal who was hoping to re-meet the girl he had met on a train in Italy the previous year, Richard, the young French writer I had met in Austria, and a host of others. We would dance at the *Club Tabou* and perhaps see Sartre sitting at a café terrace, *Les Deux Magots* or round the corner, at the *Bonaparte*. I could always ask her to come along:

hadn't she met Gide briefly in Sicily? She might be waspish, but she was not stupid, and besides, there would soon be another cheque coming from Daddy, which would certainly help matters.

I couldn't face it; I shrank from it. I imagined us all sitting at some place where the young met, like the cheaper *Royal St Germain*, across the way from *Les Deux Magots* and the *Flore*. Either she would turn on me in a tirade that would delight the more mocking of my friends or she would drop me for someone more exotic, certainly more expert, who took her fancy. Either way I would lose. I was already bruised enough almost to look forward to a period of loneliness.

My last glimpse was of her leaning against a pillar in that anonymous station. Above her head was a clock, and a sign: USCITA. She was not crying, she was not even looking, her face averted in what seemed to me now her habitual pose. It was my first adult farewell and it was a silent one. The train drew out of the station. She did not move, or wave.

> *Little white flowers*
> *will never waken you;*
> *not when the black coach*
> *of Death has taken you.*

III

The Parish of the Dead

I

'That's the last time you'll see your aunt!'

Down the hill towards the chapel came four black horses, black plumes on the two foremost, nodding like shakos. And behind them was the hearse, an oblong of polished wood, with glass sides which exposed the black solemnity of the coffin, draped with artificial flowers. On the coachman's seat perched a familiar figure, the handyman of the local undertaker, magnificently metamorphosed in frock coat and tall hat, gripping varnished reins. Behind the hearse came the mourners, relations first, discreetly silent, and then the double line of well-wishers, appearing gradually over the brow of the hill like the unwinding spool of a film. As the funeral crossed mountain roads that morning from the neighbouring valley where the dead woman had lived, the line had grown, men emerging from house or field to swell the slow-moving, quiet-talking column.

'It's a bloody big funeral, isn't it?'

'It's always big when they have to bring them to the home graveyard. One townland travels with the corpse and one meets it. They have the wake and we have the funeral.'

'We'll get paid well this morning, anyway!'

'Shut up, Stumpy; after all, it's Johnson's aunt!'

Side by side on the sacristy wall they watched, four altar boys in skimpy white surplices fringed with lace, and black soutanes which hung down against the concrete. Behind them the bulk of the post-Emancipation chapel loomed up, a barn-like building of the same pebble-dashed stone as the wall, laid out in the rough form of a cross, with a steeple over the intersection, directly above the altar, and a bell-tower near the door. Without particular distinction of feature, it yet dispensed a certain dignity, a matter of silence and shade, as though the centred reveries of a whole countryside had created a patina of peace and longing to cover its inoffensive bleakness. And around the chapel lay graves, protective railings tangled in rank grass, headstones obscured by moss and snail trails of damp; Lynch, Mellon, Carney, Kelly, Johnson, Tague, Donaghy: a whole parish lay under the clay. Only a few yards from where the boys sat, under the imitation Celtic cross of the Johnson plot, was a newly opened grave, a pile of bones and rotting coffin wood placed neatly to one side, and a shovel projecting from the mound of wet clay with the incongruous assertive gaiety of a flagpole.

'Death's very odd, isn't it? You never knew they were living until they die, and then you can hardly remember them.'

'What'll you remember about your aunt, Johnson?'

Before he had time to answer, a door opened behind them and the sacristan's head peered out.

'Boys,' he called, 'the priest's ready.'

Dropping to the ground, the boys raced to the sacristy where the priest, his robing completed, was arranging the chalice. The covering of the chalice was black and his vestments were black with a silver cross on the shoulders. As the boys filed out onto the altar, two before and two after the priest, John Johnson was still wondering what he would remember about his aunt, for whom this Mass of the Dead was being offered. She was the first of his relations to die, but already she seemed to have shrunk to little more than a presence, with that lean benevolence so typical of the women in his family, a tall bony figure who proffered apples or oranges, and caressed him, without asking where he had been or with whom, inextricable already from the gaunt figures that remained, grouped in mourning, in the front benches of this draughty chapel. As the slow tolling of the bell gathered the last of the people, the boy reflected that one thing that certainly distinguished her, for him, was the day he brought news of her illness, the day of her death.

II

All that afternoon the boy came running, running across the dusty mountain road that linked the townlands. A man working among the potato drills, a stooped figure against a background of blue sky as in a religious painting, raised his head to call: 'Where do you think you're going?' But his voice died away as the boy came under the silencing shadows of trees, and down into the hollow of the road. Then a horse, cropping the rough grass at the edge, threw up a frightened head, thrust out its great slovenly underlip, and backed wildly against the ditch. His breath harsh in his lungs, the boy drove his feet onwards with the hammered reiteration on his tongue, *Hurry, hurry, hurry.*

He passed a line of tiny County Council cottages, with windowboxes shining unexpectedly against dirty whitewashed walls. A greyhound, sniffing hungrily at the doorstep of the last, raised its pointed snout as he jogged past, and then came flying out, elongated and loping, to wander a few yards at his side and then drop back.

'O Mary, Mother of God,' he prayed, for the first time in his life feeling the words rise with real intent and urgency, rather than the accepted ritual. 'O Mary, Mother of God, let me be in time.'

He passed the last farm — a long low series of buildings, the farmhouse with greening thatch and a half-door on which a chicken roosted, the outhouses roofed with corrugated zinc and with no doors at all — and came over the brow of the hill and down onto the smooth surface of the main country road.

Elated but breathless, he halted when he came to the house. In the afternoon sunlight its long slanted roof seemed dull and unprotected, its windows facing the road like blank eyes, lit only by the occasional reflection of passing cars. Once there had been trees and outbuildings, but year by year they had fallen away, leaving the outlines of the house more exposed. As he stood, seeking to regain his breath and fumbling for the right way to convey his message, he seemed to sense the sadness of the house, from which a large family had scattered, leaving only a few survivors who gradually let the place shrink to the extent of their needs. And to this sadness, he must now add. He saw his Aunt Mary, a tall woman with loose white hair and a straggling apron, lost as always in reverie or prayer, come through the door and walk absentmindedly across his path. She was carrying a pair of hedge-clippers, and proceeded to fix the loose tendrils of a rosebush so that they hung in a pattern over the painted wooden gate leading into the farmyard.

'Aunt Mary!' he called urgently.

She turned, hearing his voice, with the puzzled uncertainty of someone already slightly deaf, and then stood, clippers in one hand, the steel points jabbing downwards, the other hand raised towards her face in an involuntary gesture of amazement at his sweat-coarsened features, dust-white shoes, and tousled hair.

'Goodness, John,' she said vaguely, 'where did you come from?'

He did not know what to say, but stood looking at her, uneasily.

'Did your father send you?'

'No,' he said, scuffing the ground with the side of his shoe.

'Your mother, then? Is there anything wrong?'

'No, it wasn't her.'

'What is it then?'

Gathering courage, he blurted: 'I've come from Aunt Margaret's. There may be something wrong with her.'

Startled, she motioned him indoors. 'Come inside and tell us about it. Martha's making tea, and you'll be able to get your breath back.'

In the dark kitchen, before the fireplace where a large black pot swung from a soot-covered crook, he found the atmosphere of intimacy he needed to speak. He sat on a sagging armchair and watched the expression change on the faces of his aunts as he explained his errand, like cloud succeeding light on an upland field.

'Some of the children going past told me Aunt Margaret wanted to see me and when I came up to the house, Uncle Malachy was leaving in the lorry for the doctor. So I went up to the room and there she was lying and when she heard me, she rose in bed and she looked very strange. She asked me to come over and see if Mary could come. And there was such a look on her face that I didn't stop running until I'm here.'

But Mary did not go after all. There was too much for her to do at home. So Martha set out, with a stick in her hand and a mongrel dog at her heels, to take the short cut across the mountains and down into the valley where the few houses of the neighbouring townland squatted along the banks of a bog-brown river. John stayed on at the house, bringing the cattle in for milking and then driving them out again into cool evening fields. Then he herded the drowsily squawking hens into their house for the night. As he moved around the farmyard in the summer twilight, hearing the rattle of buckets and the warm sound of calves shifting in an outhouse, he gradually lost his sense of strain and bewilderment, hardly even remembering the news he had brought only a few hours before. Only when he joined his aunt to say the rosary did it all come back; the words seemed to mean so much more than usual, his aunt giving them the weight and colouring of her own sorrow, as she knelt with her white hair spread on her shoulders. Was it true that she had heard the banshee when his Uncle John, the eldest son of the family, had died in America? There were pictures of him up-stairs, posed photographs in the style of the 1920s, in which he looked large and clear-eyed as an ox; Uncle John had played the fiddle and liked to drink, that was all the boy knew of him. When she came to the family prayers, his aunt added one for a special intention, which he knew to be Margaret's health. Then, shaking holy water around his shoulders and giving him a lighted candle, she told him to go to bed.

His sleep was fitful and unhappy; the memories of the day took on a new shape, grotesque and terrible. He was running on a dusty road and something was following him, filling the sky above his head, blotting out the sun. He looked up, thinking it might be only a rain cloud, but as he watched, it began to take shape, the shape of a carriage with horses travelling at a reckless speed. The horses were black, the carriage was black, but the great iron-rimmed wheels made no noise as it sped past him. He woke, crying out, to see the morning light on the bedroom wall, the emerging shape of the washstand, the tossed bedclothes. During the night, news of Margaret's death had come. The funeral would be the following day.

III

After the last gospel, the priest turned to the sacristy to remove his vestments, and emerged again in soutane and surplice, followed by the head altar boy with a collection box. It was the time for Offerings, a tradition which still survived in a few Northern parishes, whereby relations and neighbours showed their respect by contributing money in proportion to the closeness of their tie with the dead person. Since the lump sum (often as large as £50 to £100) fell to the priest saying the Mass, there was always a good deal of grumbling about the practice, and comparisons were made with more enlightened parishes where the Offerings had been stopped. But the people of Altnagore were secretly entranced by the slow ritual, beginning with the relatives (Thomas Johnson, One Pound! Mary Johnson, One Pound!) through the local merchants and strong farmers (James Devlin, Ten Shillings! Frank Mulgrew, Ten Shillings!) down to distant acquaintances and farm labourers (Dan MacNulty, Five Shillings! James Carty, Half a Crown!) It was an expression of hierarchy, fatalistically accepted, but also something more — a form of propitiation, a tribute by the parish of the living to the parish of the dead to which they in turn would belong. Even the few Protestants came to pay their respects, filing sheepishly into the back of the chapel just as the

Mass ended, in time to join the slow procession to the altar rails, their abrupt, biblical Scottish and North-country names blending for once with those of their neighbours (Sarah Wilson, Half a Crown! William Clemens, Half a Crown! Isaac MacLean, Half a Crown!)

Today it was a big Offerings, since two areas of the parish were involved and the Johnson family were known in the district. Presided over by the priest and one of the chief mourners, the long line of people, many in their working clothes, wound up and down the aisle. The chief mourner was, of course, the boy's uncle, Malachy Gorman, Margaret's husband. Properly sombre in an old-fashioned high collar with a flowing silk tie, Uncle Malachy nevertheless looked a bit strange, disquieting. It was not the colour of his suit — he generally wore black in any case — but its cut: he looked jaunty, almost dapper, like a dummy in a draper's window. He might have taken the same pose on his wedding day. And there was his expression: it was not that he did not look sad like the others, but that he looked almost contented in his sadness, taking misfortune not as a blow in the dark, but as the confirmation of his views about life. Like a seal in water, like a lark in the air, Malachy Gorman visibly revelled in his position of chief mourner. In many ways, the boy thought, the most extraordinary thing about his aunt had been her choice of husband. Now that the tie between him and the Johnson family was broken, he would probably not see Uncle Malachy very much in the future, but he would certainly remember him.

IV

It was not that his family had ever said anything in his hearing about Uncle Malachy; it was an uneasiness he sensed, rather than a definite objection. They were glad his Aunt Margaret had finally married, but they seemed to feel that she could have done better than Malachy Gorman, especially after waiting so long. Nor was it an act of desperation on her part, watching her thirties fall away; Aunt Margaret presented the same plain, lean, smiling face to the world, whether wedded or single: she seemed encased in effortless good humour. As the youngest of a large family she had received, despite the early death of her parents, more affection than most, and she saw no reason not to return the kindness. She had taken Malachy Gorman as she had taken everything else that came her way, good or ill, vaguely regarding this, her first and last proposal, as part of God's inscrutable will, part of an inevitable pattern of good.

It was not even that her husband was a 'traveller' — the local euphemistic description of a man who traded in everything from hens to old clothes to scrap iron — that troubled the family; it was rather something in his character, something exaggerated and unreal. He was monumentally gruesome. Tall, thin, lantern-jawed (but the lantern gave no light, only the blue-dark shadow of stubble), he always dressed in a black suit, with fraying cuffs, and a worn, shiny green bowler hat. Even his eyes were dark: magnificently black-irised like sloes, they gazed with voluptuous bleakness into a devastated world....

And yet it was this melancholy which made him so successful a businessman in his own peculiar line. He toured the country-side in a black Ford lorry with rattling mudguards, calling at every house and cottage. 'Any old hens today, Ma'am?' he would say, leaning his dark jaw over the half-door. He had a regular litany of dead objects which he intoned in a harsh sing-song: 'Any old clothes, any old metal, any old buckets or bed-steads?' And the woman of the house would invariably rise, even if she was in the middle of a meal, and bring him around where the hens scratched in the casual dirt of the farmyard, among old tyres and upturned buckets. By the time she returned, the dinner might have gone cold on the table, the pot on the fire boiled over, the cat tumbled the cold crocks of milk in the dairy, but the woman would hardly notice.

For the secret of Malachy Gorman's success was his ability,

as the country called it, 'to sup sorrow with a long spoon'. In him the hard-pressed farmer's wife met a real companion in misery — one who would make no attempt to raise but weigh the scales still further. Others might bring gossip or, as in the case of the doctor, a professional breeziness as a right of entrance; he responded to her long-hoarded melancholy with the professional attention of a priest bending over in the darkness of the confessional. As they moved around farmyard and outhouses, slowly and deliberately as a cortège, he would listen attentively to the long catalogue of tribulations and trials, aches and ailments, and then dextrously interpose his comment: 'Ah, yes, I know exactly how you feel, ma'am. My own cousin James had the same pain for a long time. It took him one day during the harvesting; he was nearly doubled up with the dint of it. Just below the kidneys it was. He was in bed for a month and the worst of the year, too, when all the help was needed. The wife herself had to go out to work in the fields and while she was away the cows broke into MacMahon's field and ruined their udders on the barbed wire.'

As he spoke, his gimlet eye continued to survey the landscape, estimating the amount of salvageable iron in a discarded plough, the suspicious limp of a rooster, its horny leg roughly bound with a cloth. Then, suddenly, he saw what he wanted and bent quickly down to grab some hen with trailing wings or droopy wattle. Held aloft, it squawked miserably, terror battling listlessness for a moment in its white-bleared eye, a thin stream of excrement jetting from its tail. 'That one's in a bad way, ma'am. I'd better take it off your hands before it falls apart. You'll never see another egg from that girl, not if you live till Doomsday.'

And the hen went to join a squawking assembly in a dung-soaked cage at the back of the lorry, together with a piece of old iron and a broken bedstead with sagging metal springs. When the farmyard had been gutted of everything redundant, decayed, and discarded, the lorry moved out onto the road again, top-heavy and rattling. A week later, the hens, clipped, cleaned, and briefly rejuvenated by a special diet (corn soaked nightly in whiskey, some said) and with brightly coloured strings on their legs, were dispatched to Belfast on an evening train to be sold as young juicy pullets for officers' tables. The mattress was gutted for its feathers, which were in great demand for making fleece-lined jackets for the invasion army now gathering in Ulster and remote parts of Britain. Scrap metal was also scarce; a German soldier, falling in a ditch in Normandy, would never know that, owing to Malachy Gorman's ingenuity, his life had been taken by a piece of Maggie Devlin's bedstead in the shape of a bullet. (As for Maggie Devlin, had she known the chain of cause and effect, she would have prayed for the poor man all her life.) The remains, a soaked and ripped mattress cover, a crazy tangle of wire and springs, fragments of rotting wood, went to swell the great mound of rubbish that gradually rose behind Malachy Gorman's house, dwarfing it like a pyramid.

So engrossed did he appear in his sombre but highly rewarding task, that people had been very surprised when Malachy married; one did not associate him with such ideals of happiness. But Margaret Gorman, née Johnson, seemed quite contented with her new position: she worked on with quiet and diligence as she had done all her life until, bearing out her husband's view of life, she died, in her third year of marriage, after a brief illness. Happiness, in the ordinary sense, did not seem Malachy Gorman's destiny.

V

After the funeral there was the ceremonial breakfast; funerals, like weddings, brought together relatives and friends. There was his father, Thomas Johnson, restless as he watched yet another good harvest-day squander its sunlight outside the window. There was Uncle Francis, who had given up farming to keep a pub in Clogher; prematurely grey, he spoke little, but whistled continually through his teeth. There was Cousin Michael, now a parish priest in a small town in Armagh, the orchard county; he generally brought the children apples — Beauty of Bath and Bramley seedling — but not today. And there were his aunts: the married like Frances and Brigid, who had come with their husbands, one a schoolmaster from Cork, the other a cattle dealer from Westmeath; the unmarried, like Mary and Martha, who still lived in the house where they had been born, and Aunt Lucy, who was in a convent in Newry and was also called Sister Bernadette.

At first, everyone seemed uneasy, as though chilled by the long morning at the funeral and in the chapel, and by the sensation of returning, through a receding mechanism of time, to the place in which most of them had been brought up. Perspectives of childhood mocked them at every turn. Above their heads was a blackened bullet-hole where Michael Johnson, wrestling with the boy's father for possession of the rifle, accidentally fired a shot through the roof. For days the family had lived in fear in case the shot had been heard and the illegal possession of the rifle discovered. There was a picture of their father, a great white beard clouding on his chin, and their mother, a plain woman, tightly corseted. Almost involuntarily their eyes rested on these things, though without attempting to share a melancholy which each probably thought restricted to himself.

Only the children were obviously excited, scurrying from room to room, watching the chicken and the ham being prepared, smelling the strange tang of whiskey in the air. And slowly conversation sprang to remarks about the funeral, souvenirs of the dead woman, each memory rounded off with a dying fall: 'I never dreamt she'd go so quick!' It was stimulated still further by the bustling arrival of a group of latecomers. James Gormley, the undertaker, restless and dapper, his narrow breast encircled by an elaborate gold chain, moved from group to group, announcing briskly: 'It was a great Offering. Margaret Gorman was a highly regarded woman.' The parish priest,

Father Donnelly, an enormous mottled frog of a man, eased himself with accustomed sobriety into the sombre pool of the conversation: 'Margaret Gorman was a fine woman. I only hope we all have as holy and happy an end as Margaret Gorman.'

Gradually, as whiskey and companionship warmed them, the conversation widened. There was even subdued laughter. Father Donnelly told how, at a clerical conference recently, anxious to leave early, he looked for his hat, only to be confronted with an avalanche of similar black hats. One priest, however, had anticipated the problem — the lining of a hat he picked up contained the legend in large letters: LEAVE IT ALONE, DAMN YOU, IT'S NOT YOURS. Taking courage from the priest's example, the schoolmaster from Cork gave a colourful account of a recent election in his county, where the candidates had come to blows. ''Twas as good as a hurling final,' he ended, with a smack of the lips. Everyone laughed.

That was only one side of the room, however. On the other side, the boy saw his aunts sitting in a sad row, like hens sheltering from the rain, their eyes glazed with memory. And before them stood Malachy Gorman, a glass of mineral water in his hand. His head, unaccustomedly bare, showed a bald patch on the crown, bleak as a soft-shelled egg. And above the clink of glasses and the increasingly robust laughter the boy heard his voice: 'I knew it could never last. We were doing too well. Only last Easter, Margaret said that now we were making more money than we ever had, we should build a new wing to the house. The war was very good to us, you know. But I knew it couldn't last. And then I was driving over the Hill Road one evening. I saw a hearse coming towards me, it was travelling at a great rate and just as I was wondering what poor soul it could be, I saw there was no coachman in the box. Mother of God, said I, and I blessed myself as it passed, without the creak of a wheel. And when I looked after, it was gone, not a thing in sight down the whole stretch. And I knew then something was going to happen. *We were doing too well.*'

In the clucked but unsurprised assent of women's voices the boy remembered and recognised his dream. Now that he had come to know death, such dreams might recur, hints of that mortality he shared with everyone in the room. But he hoped he wouldn't be frightened by them. For some people, he would discover, death, contemplated too long and too lovingly, became almost a reason for existence; although they sometimes consoled others, they ended by becoming monstrous figures themselves, almost comic in their obsession. Hearing the boy behind him, Malachy Gorman turned, showing a smile as brief and purposefully bright as the cutting blade of a MacCormick reaper. The boy smiled uneasily in return. Then he turned away, reluctantly, to the other side of the room, where his father was calling him.

The Three Last Things

Mrs Hanger was dying. In the whole village everyone knew it; but then she (and her taciturn, gloomy husband) had been there ten years. And during that decade she had entered into the ordinary life of the community, chatting to the old, playing with the young, sipping an occasional sherry in Sheila's pub. If she was not one of their own, something no outsider could ever hope to be, she was certainly no 'blow in', as an angry Irish leader had once defined it; she was as close to being accepted as anyone had come. They loved her openness, her warmth and lack of malice, the cheerfulness of her brown American face: *God love her.*

Besides, Castlehobble was not an ordinary town. It was beside the sea, but it was not a resort. You might cycle or drive out to some quiet cove, or boat out to one of the islands, but it did not have the garish, sun-worshipping life of the modern seaside. People went to fish, people swam (naked even, when they found a deserted island beach) but Castlehobble was not especially interested in bronzed summer visitors, speaking strange languages, and striding half nude down the main street, garlanded with dangling cameras, tentacled walkmans. They might drink in the one fashionable pub, or buy out the new delicatessen line in the grocery store, but Castlehobble only smiled at them, from an incurious distance. It had its own way of life, its own gait of going, to which they were irrelevant, as unreal as tropical birds that had blundered onto a chilly coast.

That was why Martha's dying meant so much to them — she was the one foreigner they had nearly taken to their bosom, so to speak. For if the Hangers were not natives, born and bred to the bare rock, neither were they migrants, who might up and disappear when the first cold tipped their wings. Had she (and again, as an afterthought, they added her husband) not lived out the long winter months when the town was swathed in a constant mist, or squalls of rain, and the foghorn on the point could be heard, wailing like some disconsolate beast? Then they became a real community, living in and through each other, organising whist drives, dinners, dances, Old People's Evenings and children's games, usually in the splendid Community Hall which her husband had helped design for them. A local wit had dubbed it Happiness Hanger, a description that would hardly apply to the glum, lean face of its designer. The son of a clergyman, legend had it, in which case he was living proof that, like their own priests (Father Ger, for example), servants of God should remain celibate, offer it up.

Ten winters she had endured with them, weaving spells of friendship and gossip against the driving wind and wet, the claustrophobia of that remote Western coast. And now, when she was dying, they were forbidden the house — well, not quite forbidden but not expected to call too often, or without warning. For that was the practice of the community, dropping in on each other with the latest news, a pregnancy, a marriage, an impending law case. But this simplicity had its own strictness, an order in disorder, which could be violated.

The town had a new police officer, for example, a zealous young man just out of training school, whom they nicknamed the Sheriff, because of the way he kept his thumbs hooked in his regulation belt. He also had broken the unspoken rules of Castlehobble by checking driving licences, or, worse, waiting in the darkness outside public houses or private parties to arrest stumbling citizens sleepwalking towards their cars. There had rarely been an accident in Castlehobble where people knew their way home, even in the blackest nights of winter, by a kind of alcoholic radar, the seventh sense of drunkenness. To fail to understand this showed that the young guard, Seán Wayne, as they derisively called him, was only a city slicker who had confused the real and the Wild West.

All this Martha understood, for she was a real and sympathetic listener, who fathomed how small, homely details should be woven into a saga. And there were the more intimate problems of health; only a desert father or Himalayan fakir would have endured the insidious chills of winter in Castlehobble without murmur. Colds, chilblains, rheumatics, arthritis, hacking coughs and constant flus with all their attendant remedies — did she not know about them all? She had become a dab hand at their favourite anodyne for all ills: the white lightning of illegal alcohol served up hot with cloves and home-made honey. Yes, they had become accustomed to telling, even showing, their troubles to her, swollen veins and cracking joints, shingles and ringworm, yet now, in her hardest hour, they were expected not to share her own sufferings.

The wise women of the village all decided, in a close session in Sheila's snug, that it must be the fault of her husband, but it was not as simple as that. Knute Hanger might be a tall, lean foreigner who spoke to no one unless his wife was present to warm the occasion, but that was not the reason for the sudden withdrawal. Nor was it a clash of custom; the Irish habit of *céillithe*, of dropping in unexpectedly for a chat and a jar, against the formality of European manners: pre- and post-prandial drinks, the carefully maintained fortress of the family circle. No, the real reason was religion; but the kind of religion Castlehobble was least able to understand — the Hangers were both, by conviction and choice, practising atheists.

Castlehobble was an easy-going community, and proud of being so; it was definitely not one of the old priest-ridden parishes of the West, where the sins of the flesh were excoriated regularly from the altar, blasted, then beaten from the hedges by the parish priest's blackthorn. There was a small Protestant community treated as near normal by their Catholic neighbours: all farmers, sharing the vagaries of wind and weather; had they not endured the Famine together? There was a large artists' colony (potters, painters, an Australian poet with bog-Irish ancestors, who preferred Cork and Kerry to Canberra, a sculptor who hammered out large erotic abstracts, massive lingams of steel that people preferred not to comprehend) but most of these 'blow ins' were Irish, and had presumably started off life as Catholics, like everybody else. So they knew the code of their neighbours, and if they had long, friendly arguments with them, playing cards or drinking, they still knew how to watch their words, not to cross the tactful threshold of religious belief.

Only a few miles away, at Ballylicken, superstition flourished, and religion reigned. A statue of the Virgin in the roadside grotto had been seen to move, though as the crowds swelled through one summer her mobility became less obvious. Then a gravedigger had discovered an uncorrupted body in the local cemetery, 'the two eyes smiling straight up at me,' he explained emphatically in the public house that evening. The young corpse, it seemed, had been a living saint, a sweet-tempered child who died early, consumed by innumerable maladies, yet with the name of God always on her lips. Or so claimed her now elderly remaining sister who had all but forgotten her existence until she rose up again, so to speak, in the graveyard.

Castlehobble had no such special favours from the Almighty but it kept an open mind; there was an annual pilgrimage to Lourdes, which was greatly enjoyed, but as much for the wine and the *craic* as for the religious consolation. But to ignore both church and chapel and declare that God could not, did not, exist was something else. In the long memory of the village it had happened only the once, when someone had harmlessly asked Knute Hanger which church he favoured, what religion his country or region practised.

'None, thank God,' he had answered curtly and then, in case there should be any misunderstanding, added with a wrathful urgency which belied his usual sullenness and silence: 'I do not hold with such rubbish. Why should we invent a Being to blame for our own beastliness?' And as his interlocutor shrank away before this sudden explosion, Knute advanced on his hapless victim. 'If he does exist, then he is, as you say here, *a right bastard*,' was Knute's final salute, mistaking an expression of total shock for one of religious anguish, an emotion not preva-lent in Castlehobble, or indeed in the whole country.

So in Sheila's pub they discussed the situation in whispers. 'She's not well at all,' said Sheila, 'and sinking daily.'

'I don't like the look of her; she's not long for this world,' echoed her sister; between them they laid out all the female corpses of the village and would, it seemed, lay out Martha before long, with all the ancient and impassive skill of their kind. In preparation for which they had been admitted to the bedside; but the astonishing thing was that they had gone, not on some tiptoeing errand, but at Martha's specific request, as old friends from whom she would shortly be requiring a last service. Such lack of mystery or false modesty, such matter-of-fact clarity about death was something totally unexpected and alien to Castlehobble, more accustomed to the solemn tones of the panegyric or the wakehouse eulogy. Surely the end was not like closing down a shopfront, or shutting a gap; just a formality, a shade harsher than most because of the pain involved? But even that seemed to be scanted, for as Sheila said, 'She won't talk much about her sickness at all, and when she does speak, she's clear as a bell.'

And her sister added: 'You'd never guess from her face what she was going through, although of course she's nearly grey and light as a ghost. Talk about soldiers — she'd show them how to die any day. The bold Knute wouldn't face the firing squad as lightly.'

The other women listening agreed, with secret pangs of envy and admiration, for, after all, the sisters had been allowed to see such a paragon of their sex's proverbial powers of endurance. And they swallowed hungrily any scraps of information about Martha's state, both of body and mind, while feeling terribly cheated. Like actors summoned to a modern version of a classical tragedy, relegated from the solemn and mournful responses of the chorus to the sideline, they felt oddly useless, somehow insulted in their final, traditional role as sympathetic witnesses of human destiny. Funerals had changed since the old days when whole families would pray the dying into the next world, preparing the wake while waiting for the last gasp, soothing the brow while setting out the whiskey and snuff, but such hygienic death, such a clinical withdrawal, like a curtain drawn in a hospital ward, was more like New York than Castlehobble. Why had the Hangers chosen to live there if they chose to ignore its most cherished feelings about what an old Irish poet had described as the three last things?

'And how is Knute taking it?' they enquired with carefully phrased indifference. As far as they were concerned, he was the real stumbling block, the spanner in the works, who must ultimately be to blame for his wife's sudden severity of attitude. For he defeated all their expectations, in looks, dress and behaviour: dignified as a senior clergyman, like his father probably; they still did not know what to make of him, especially when he had dropped his guard so abruptly once, shown his savagely secular hand. That such a serious man should deny the existence of God was impossible; most of the educated men of their world, priests and teachers, were specifically dedicated to upholding religion. And Knute looked more like them than they did themselves — never a breath of scandal, never a savage bout of drunkenness, but always so soberly dressed, with his neat beard and dark clothes. And so courteous, bowing to every woman he met on the street, all the assembled friends or least acquaintances of Martha, as if they were ladies from some dignified past. How could you have the manners of a gentleman and not believe in the Supreme Being? And behave with such deference to womankind if you were not prepared to recognise, to accept their humble, centuries-old effort to share His suffering, under the banner of the one true God, who had shown us how to accept death?

If He had hung in shame and pain on the good wood, bared

his man's body to the savagery of the Roman soldiers, and the taunts of the Jews, then they should bring his consolation to their dying friend, defy the terrible paganism of her husband, speed another soul towards heaven.

* * *

In Ralph's (pronounced Rave's) American Bar the menfolk gathered to discuss the situation, in the intervals of watching a re-run of a World Championship fight on the television.

'It's not right, it's not natural, it's not how things are done,' said the boss, a squat, close-cropped man who had spent years in the NYPD, New York's Finest. Ralph's was a good pub, with a sophisticated range of drinks, a diversity of taste the owner had brought back with him. Tequila, Cretan Raki, Bastida de Cao, Cassis, Cinzano, Saint Raphael, Pastis, Vermouth, Ricard, Metaxa, Ouzo and Floc de Gascoigne — you could find them all lining the higher shelves of the bar, behind the usual chubby Paddy or Powers whiskey bottles. People rarely asked for them but Ralph liked to have them there, to remind him of his wilder days in New York, and they made good opening gambits in casual conversation with impressed visitors.

But if there was a touch of cosmopolitan ease about Ralph's Bar there was also an atmosphere of subdued hostility: you either agreed with the owner or you got out; he did not like, could not bear, to be contradicted.

'She should have a proper wake, and a proper funeral,' he declared, pulling a slow luxurious pint, with its priestly collar of froth. 'It's the way it was always done here, for saint or sinner.' His listeners did not query his knowledge of either state, for the flare of his temper was feared and famous. When his dander was up, he would have struck a saint, or emptied a pint over a priest. Meanwhile, oblivious to Ralph's theological views, George Foreman was sinking to the canvas on that hot night in Zaire, surely never to rise in glory again, psyched out by Cassius Clay, now known as Mohammed Ali.

* * *

Knute Hanger gazed out through his dining room window at the light dying on the Atlantic. He had always loved the sea, its squalls and smiles, that continually changing presence, which he could see from every window of the house in which he had chosen to live. Rather he and Martha, the son of a German pastor and the daughter of a German Jewish survivor of the pogroms.

For years after the war they had searched the world for some outpost of uncomplicated kindness. Southern Mexico had seemed right for a time, but they got tired of being called 'gringo' by the children in the marketplace, and Martha had discovered that prices doubled when she entered the local shops, and although she addressed them in fluent Spanish, they always answered in broken English, forcing them back to the Yankee ghetto.

And so they tried Ireland, moving further and further west, until they found this harbour home. Here in this damp extremity of Europe, they had found a haven, the paradoxical ideal of a gregarious isolation. The town of Castlehobble received them, but also left them discreetly alone. There were the long conversations with the locals in the shops and public houses but no one intruded, while responding cheerfully to any overture. And there were enough artists to ensure a minimum of technical exchange, if Knute was going through a bad period. Yes, on the whole, it had been fruitful; for a decade of loving peace, during which he had painted some of his best pictures, and Martha had raised her children, and come to know and love the village, warily at first, but with a gathering appreciation of the web the locals spun around every incident in the endless saga of Castlehobble.

And now their union was being broken up, by the dictates of a cruel fate, their love was being extinguished. There were only a few gleams of light left, far out at sea, as Knute softly quoted to himself famous lines from *King Lear*: 'As flies to wanton boys are we to the gods; they kill us for their sport.' There could not be a God, whatever historians said about our advance from polytheism, the multitudinous deities of the Greeks and Indians, because if there was one central Being, then he was a blind monster, whom one could only loathe.

Take his most intelligent, loving, but now dying wife. Why create such a delicate, affectionate, thinking creature only to destroy it? Such a death was the ultimate absurdity, an affront to life. If God existed, he was to blame for having devised this cruel charade, and not only for single human beings, however valuable, but on a grand scale. Contemplating the full horror of the twentieth century — death camps and atomic bombs — if God existed, he must be a sadist, for allowing such things to happen. Bad enough that mankind should die, as Martha was now doing, but not stripped, humiliated, broken down by pain or torture.

That was the dilemma of free will, of course, but he agreed that it was better to blame the bestiality of some men than invent some all-powerful Aztec entity who sat back, accepting these rivers of blood as homage, or reclined on his golden throne, deaf to the cries of suffering beneath him. Instead of a medieval vision of Christ the King, who would separate the sheep from the goats, the Elect from the Damned, Knute Hanger, son of Pastor Hanger, heard these cries of anguish, saw the stumbling hordes of victims, whose supplications ascended endlessly into the void. The twentieth century was an Inferno with no hint of a Paradiso; why kid yourself, as the Americans said, when with fire and brimstone, as in the Old Testament, man blasted his fellow man, was, indeed, prepared to blast the very earth itself? If the Christian God of these Irish peasants, and his learned father, really existed, then he was to be hated and dethroned immediately. Any so-called parent would step in if he saw his child mistreating even a dog; the way Martha had tended a whole zoo of ailing animals, cats, mongrels, donkeys beaten or deserted by their owners. But God the Father showed no compassion, only the blind face of indifference; the latest example being the way his beloved wife was being broken down, cell by dying cell. He was right to have declared war against the Christian fallacy as early as he could, disbelieving for the same reasons his father believed.

* * *

Knute Hanger's father had been a Lutheran pastor in an industrial town in North Germany, near the Baltic. He remembered his study, its deep stillness, like a cellar or a well, the simple cross on the table, the few Dürer etchings on the walls. But mainly books, the complete works of the great philosophers, like Emmanuel Kant, the poets like Goethe and Schiller, a copy of Luther's *Heilige Schrift* on a lectern. He had browsed there for hours when he was a boy, devouring the Old Testament for its wonderful stories of war and lust and high adventure, Daniel in the Lions' Den, or the boy David defying Goliath.

Yet it was in that tranquil atmosphere that he had at last to confront his pastor father. It had begun at school where so many of his schoolmates had joined the Hitler Jugend. Knute was against it but his father felt it would be wiser not to make a fuss. Young and all as he was, Knute discovered in himself a rage that he did not know he was capable of; he ended up shouting at the pastor.

'You believe, Father, that I should follow these puppets, as they strut like their stupid fathers. Little bullies, in a few years they will be swilling beer, and boasting, like that horrible fatso, Goering. Surely your son should behave better? I am proud to be a scholar, like you, and besides, I loathe uniforms.'

His father tried to explain that there were historical reasons for what was happening.

'It's that Treaty is to blame, and the shame of Weimar. Germans feel humiliated; they want to show that they are not broken, they are still men.'

'A uniform doesn't make a man better; do we respect a postman or ticket collectors more than others? No, the Nazis want to march together like maniacs, saluting that little counter-jumping lunatic from Austria, with the false name.'

'You are unfair: the Nazi Party has helped to give Germany back its pride. Versailles was an act of revenge, not a peace pact. We raise an army again, and the world respects Germany again.'

'Respect, my eye, he will lead us to Wagnerian perdition, your Chancellor. Look how he has already cowed your people; are you proud of the Reich Church? Have you heard of Pastor Bonhoeffer's professorship at his seminary being terminated? Or does he not count, because he is not an Orthodox Lutheran? Maybe he should learn Luther's gift for abuse.'

His father went silent, gazing around at his library, so proudly accumulated from Gymnasium days. He was a fine man, but the theological works he loved to peruse — Busching, Bauer, Kaehler on the Historical Jesus — were of no use to him now, confronting his brilliant son, an adolescent hurled into harsh maturity. It was only the first of many sharp exchanges, the last being when Knute announced his decision not to come to church any more, because of what he regarded as his father's cowardice. It was after service and the kapellmeister was running through a fugue in the background. The pastor had timidly suggested that instead of denouncing *Mein Kampf*, as his son wished him to do, one should consider the good ideas in it.

'Like his views on the Jews, written largely by Streicher? Are they alone to be blamed for the inequality of the German economy? We should be our own scapegoat.'

But his father still prevaricated and Knute could stand it no longer.

'If good men like you stand by, then we are lost. Or maybe your Church is at fault: I've been reading Luther in your library, and he abused the Jews because they didn't convert.'

'That was late in his life. The Jews have always suffered: it is their race's destiny. But you know Psalm 126 quoted in Brahms' *Deutsches Requiem*: "they that sow in tears shall reap in joy." There is a larger pattern which you are too young to discern.'

Joy indeed. He saw the stormtroopers at work in the Jewish ghetto, prodding a bearded Hasidic rabbi forwards with a bayonet, reviling children, smashing old shop windows. Should the old Christ-killers have turned the other cheek, like true Christians?

Some dark cloud now hung over the world, deforming men into Bosch-like creatures, fanged wolves, murderous insects, drinkers of blood who showed a cannibalistic delight in mangling human flesh and bone. In the Middle Ages there had been the dreaded Plague; during the Reformation the Wars of Religion. But neither malady nor religion could be produced as an excuse for what was happening in their own fatherland. So there and then he had decided that the God his father prayed to could not, did not, exist, if he were to make any sense out of contemporary life, which violently proclaimed God's absence, his desertion, his disappearance. Knute Hanger left home, slipping across the border into Denmark, then making his way to England when the war broke out. In due course, as his reward, he would be amongst the first Allied soldiers to enter Dachau. He still kept a photograph on his desk as a souvenir of that day, the final incontrovertible proof of man's latent savagery, contradicted only by the sweetness of generous spirits like his now bravely dying wife.

* * *

Martha Hanger had arranged to be alone, one hour in the morning, one in the afternoon, one after dinner, so that she could compose her declining energies to face her problem. Her problem, she thought ironically, her demise, her sudden disappearance, an abrupt leaving of all the small details of her life; daily she wrote goodbye notes to distant friends. Her favourite books surrounded her on the bed, mainly poetry, because she would never again have time to immerse herself in the structure of a novel, to interest herself in the loves and hates of fictional characters. Poetry lay in small piles on either side of her, or at the foot of the bed, the thick bulk of a Collected, single volumes as slim as devotional or political pamphlets. Which, of course, they were, in a sense, manifestos about living and loving, from the darkness of Paul Celan to the quivering self-regard of Rilke, the thunder of Thomas. Each one offered her a different vision and, according as she weakened or wavered, she could reach for the psychic shock of their particular truth. How could you reconcile the measured tones of the vice-president of the Hartford Insurance Company intoning that 'life contracts and death is expected, / As in a season of autumn. / The Soldier falls' with the angry outcry of Dylan (they had met him in the White Horse in 1952, dishevelled but full of aggressive grief for his dying father) that we should 'not go gentle into that good night'? If she raged against her fate, she did it, as she had done most things in her life, gently, calmly, with consideration for others. She admired the fury of the drunken Welsh gnome but her upbringing gave her more in common with the Connecticut recluse.

Tiring of poetry, or writing last letters, she could look up to contemplate the pictures she had chosen to keep as lifetime companions on the walls of her bedroom. There were the Irish works acquired during the last decade, mostly traditional glimpses of Castlehobble life, an old man battering his stubborn donkey along, a proud fisherman holding up a gleaming fish, a study of a sparrowhawk, or kestrel swooping over a small animal. There was a hint of menace in some of these studies by local artists, the teeming hedge life that went on relentlessly under the lichened stones and dripping, cloudy skies when the warm evening was full of owl calls, the rustle of fleeing prey.

But they were meek, almost soothing beside the strange abstracts of her husband, canvases covered with slashes of dark paint, or dripping with colours like tears running down a raddled face. How well she knew the brooding that had gone into them, days, weeks, months on end as Knute wrestled with the void which, for him, underlay the living world. He could not sleep, he prowled the house talking and crying to himself until the tension eased, with some temporary victory or stay against the cannibal darkness. She did not feel as strongly about things as he did, but she accepted his views: was she not the daughter of someone who had nearly died in the camps he had helped to liberate?

His cartoons were now famous, a post-Holocaust version of George Grosz, an assembly line of black humour with small men being savaged by giant spouses, who were subjugated in their turn by phallic machines: the sexual cruelty of modern war and modern life was systematically exploited in a horrifying but palatable way. The very people who were being satirised — gaunt American hostesses with rings sparkling on every finger — rushed to buy them, in an extravagant act of self-castigation. The baby seal bleeding on the ice with a New York Maenad standing over his tiny carcass, screaming, 'I want that fur for Tuesday's party at the Strumpfs', hubby!' had become a signature for the Conservation Lobby. And the divorcing couple slicing everything in two, their palatial house, their car, their pets, and finally their children, with war cries of: 'And now are you satisfied?'

She preferred less obvious drawings, which detailed the little cruelties of nature, a heron stilting with a still-living fish in his slender beak, the heron which lived in a misty pool where the river debouched in the sea. They went by to see him on clear evenings and were rewarded sometimes to see His Eminence, as they called him, gain the rewards of his patience. And there was a clutch of gannets offshore which would dive past the boat with that undeviating marvellous line of speed, striking the still water (for they could not spy their target otherwise) with their beaks, with a sound like a quick clap. Observing nature, he was un-paralleled in his loving exactness: a spiky whirl of evening swallows, all beaks and claws and tiny wingbeats, a badger they had met on the road, loping along, head low, all hunched up. And the hedgehogs he brought home, to feed with a spoon and scraps from the table, as he did the baby birds. How could this tenderness coexist with his stridency, his satirical harshness; perhaps because he could not harm a butterfly himself he was horrified by the nonchalance of those who did?

He was a loving, caring but most complicated man, and perhaps the loneliness of the abstracts was closest to his real self. She knew how deep they came from inside her husband's psyche, an attempt to describe where no description was possible, to sound the rhythm of darkness that beat all night under the skies and seas of the world. Done in rage, vexation, near despair, they were the testimonies of a supremely honest spirit. If Nihil, not even Satan, or Lucifer, the fiery fallen, was in charge of the universe, then every work of art was a gesture against its black power, a throw of the dice in a game that had no meaning. It could not be denied, but must be fought, to the bitter end.

How much of the old Protestant pastor still lay within him, with unbelief as his belief! It was a position that God, if he existed, would pity and understand — the God of the New Testament. There had to be genuine unbelievers, people in whom the apparently useless appendix of belief was missing. She had never forgotten his description of entering Dachau, the yellow smoke from miles away, the sudden hush of the jubilant troops, the figures scrabbling at the wire; the ultimate insult to the nostrils, the smell of the charnel house. Heartsick, fumbling, their marching pride reduced to silence, the liberating troops had offered presents to their skeletal greeting party but their bodies rejected even C-rations immediately.

She could see all this behind his paintings and in their dark way they brought her some comfort. For it was into that darkness she was sinking. Each day she sank a little bit further away from it all, like a waterlogged boat. The disease had already reached her lower limbs; she had never thought she would see the day when she could not wiggle her toes but it was already there and climbing towards her knees. The doctor and the specialists had said that the whole process would take a month and that it was irreversible; she would die slowly upwards, her brain wearily clear until the poisons engulfed her whole system.

There is nothing clears the mind like a sentence of death; she had found the old Johnsonian cliché true for her. For what could she do to distract herself from the anguish, the pitiless facts? She did not drink much, and although the doctor offered her drugs, she took them only when the pain was devouring; it was constant and inexorable but not unbearable. The last few days might be difficult: she had discussed with her Irish doctor a special cocktail of drugs which would, he said, make St Lawrence hornpipe on his gridiron, and at that ultimate point between death and life, dissolution and reality, she felt she might be allowed some hilarity. In the meantime, she set herself as bravely as she could, for the sake of her husband as well, to die the way they had lived, with the stern humility of rational humanism. Sweetened, in her case, by poetry; she reached down for one of her favourite volumes and began to chant to herself the slight but singing lines she already knew so well. 'What answer but endurance, kindness / Against her choice, I still affirm / That nothing dies....'

Consoling words, but were they true? She would soon be in a position to find out. She heard the murmur of voices through the door, the voice of her husband, the voice of the local parish priest, Father Gerard O'Driscoll, Ger for short. He had called up Knute early in the month, with tentative courtesy. He had not been officially informed but the whole village was following her rapid descent with such fascination that he could not help knowing about it. So he proceeded with all due ceremony, phoning beforehand, setting an exact hour for his visit. And he arrived with a bottle under his arm, a bottle of Schnapps from Ralph's Bar, for he knew his host's taste. Many's the winter evening they had spent, playing chess, and drinking quietly, as the waves lapped against the harbour wall, the light died from the porthole windows, and the winds strained the rafters, until the room creaked like the cabin of a ship at sea.

Knute Hanger received the gift in silence and set out two neat glasses. After the third application of the dry, sharp spirits the priest felt free to speak.

'There is no hope, then?'

'None.'

'How long does she have?'

'Four, five days, maybe a week. It goes fast in the final stages.'

'May I see her?'

Knute was silent for a while, then he threw back, rather than swallowed, a swift Schnapps.

'As long as you don't try to sneak in any prayers. She should die as she has lived. No fooling around with rosary beads or holy water; absolutely no false promises about the next life, compassionate judges and flapping angels. It is not our style.'

It was the priest's turn to be silent and apply himself to the Schnapps. He liked Knute, with whom he had spent so many pleasant evenings (they were now equally matched in chess, Knute's early skill grown rusty in the Irish air, the priest using long, lonely hours to practise in his presbytery). And he liked his directness, so bracingly different from the calculated vagueness of so many of his Irish parishioners, who approached a subject as if it were a hare hidden in a thicket. But this evening Knute was more brusque than ever, under the pressure of this new trial, this new proof, the priest realised, of all the worst that he feared and felt about life. They had discussed that too, near the end of the bottle, but theological exchange was not in order, when simple human compassion was needed.

'Of course not,' he said, draining his glass. 'I just want to say a straight goodbye. We worked together a lot, you know, in the charity area. A very genuine woman, always glad to help, no matter what our differences of opinion might have been. We were always open with each other.'

He could not prevent an embarrassed sharpness creeping into his own comments.

Knute hung his head, hopelessly.

'In you go. She's expecting you. When she heard you had telephoned, she particularly asked to see you. I said it would be pointless, that you couldn't help but try and lure her, that it was your bounden duty to twitch the thread, that you were a priest first, and a friend afterwards. I know your sort.'

Father O'Driscoll was silent. The diagnosis was not far from the mark and, once again, as in many previous exchanges, he had to register the man's honesty. It came hard to Knute to speak harshly, the priest could see, but he said what he felt had to be said, no matter what the circumstances. Would to God — there he went again — his parishioners could manage such probity. But Knute had already read his silence as hurt.

'I know,' he said flatly, 'I know because of my father; he had to preach, too. He believed, against all the evidence, that even I had a Christian soul which had to be saved, against my will. He thought that all suffering could be explained if it led us to Christ: that even the poor tortured victims of Nazidom might achieve baptism by desire, expire in such pain that it brought them close to what the Portuguese call The Man. You remind me of him sometimes, when you speak of your straying parishioners. In a good-humoured way, of course, Father, but I can feel the hunter, the heavenly fisherman, biding his time, and I resent him. That baited hook hung over my childhood soul. There have been tyrants before, and bad times, but there is only one God. I despise and resent such single-minded sophistry. My soul, immortal or mortal, is not a fish, nor am I a brand to be plucked from the burning; your God loves cruel metaphors.'

'And you have been squirming on his hook ever since,' thought Father O'Driscoll, but he withheld his comment. What in heaven — there he went again — did he know about the whole process, despite what they had taught him in the seminary? He learned from his life, with the staff of his belief to help him. With a last swift snort of Schnapps he headed for the sickroom, and for the strangest deathbed exchange of his pastoral life so far.

* * *

Father Ger O'Driscoll was used to death, and deathbeds; they were as much part of his daily rounds as of a doctor's. Confessions at the weekend were not as regular as they used to be and even Mass attendance had dwindled a little. At first he had been inclined to blame the influx of artists into the community, which was becoming an Irish branch of St Ives, but he knew they had very little effect on his flock, most of whom were blind to them, even the erotic drawings of John Lucy, with their oriental application to the details of lovemaking.

It was more likely to be mere laziness, staying up at night to look at 'The Late Late Show' on television, or some horrible Hollywood soap opera. How often had he dropped into a farmhouse and found them sitting in darkness, not facing the heat of the stove, or murmuring the rosary, but watching two TV stars grapple on the coloured screen. Teenage sex, lust, abortion, homosexuality, incest: they knew about all now, in theory at least, as it washed into their own kitchens all the way from Los Angeles. They turned it off for him, but the conversation was stiff, until he indicated he was keeping up with Gay Byrne and Jackie Collins and the other real stars of their nightly firmament. Even the ads exposed breasts and crotches to old bachelors who had never seen either; why did they never mention them in confession?

Still, he was always called for at the end, even by the most hardened. As a matter of fact, he thought grimly, his hand on the doorknob, it is nearly my most successful role, a sort of Holy Meals on Wheels, the Oils. And with a start, he remembered that he had automatically brought along his reticule (what a local quilter called his 'heavenly sowing basket') in the car, in case it might come in handy. He opened the sickroom door.

After all his years tending the sick, he was still not prepared for what he saw. Martha was propped up in bed, reading the *Collected Poems* of an Irish poet, which he had given her shortly after they had installed themselves in Castlehobble, and realised that they shared common interests. She looked weary, waxen, but her eyes were bright.

'How are you, Martha?' he asked and could have cursed his blatant stupidity.

'Surprisingly well,' she said. 'Although I have, of course, lost the control of my lower body. No feeling in my toes, none in my legs, and now it is creeping inch by inch, strictly on schedule. But as deaths go, it is an easy enough one, I suppose. At least I can keep my head, say goodbye to my friends forever, and observe death's progress. An easier journey outward than many you will have seen, Father; *poor people.*'

Even dying, her thought was of others who had suffered more. Automatically he found himself looking around for holy pictures, as in the majority of the sickrooms he visited. But instead there were drawings and paintings, particularly the strange, dark visions of her husband. He could not profess to understand the large, weeping abstracts, Veronica's veils with no divinity shadowed in them, but they had a powerful aura, which always made the priest shiver, as if contemplating slivers of the stricken psyche, the Godhead in pieces.

'So this is our last meeting,' Martha Hanger said, almost with a laugh as she saw Father O'Driscoll start with dismay before her brisk honesty. 'Unless there is one of your miracles, of course, as in dear Ballylicken. But I doubt if I will be singled out for such an honour. And I hope you have not come to convert me. Knute has probably warned you off. As the tree falls, so should it lie: I should die as I have lived.' She corrected herself. 'As we have lived.'

Ger O'Driscoll was silent. Nothing in his seminary training or his pastorate had prepared him for this; it was certainly the most direct deathbed exchange he had ever had, with the victim more convinced than the Christian pastor who had come to succour her. And yet, he knew from his experience, she must be afraid. He had tended all sorts, old mountainy men and women whose faith was as simple as spring water, notorious drunks who had craved oblivion, but nearly all died hard, till he brought them to some kind of resignation before the inevitable. He still remembered the wail of a tough old crone from the back of beyond, with the rosary beads clamped around her fist, as she rocked to and fro, crying into the winter night: 'There's a cold wind and a long road before me, and me not knowing where I go.'

'And don't you feel afraid?' he ventured, finally.

'Doesn't everyone?' countered Martha briskly. 'I have seen many of my family die, and now it is my turn. I must not cry out against our common fate. I die at home, with my husband, not butchered by the roadside, or tortured, or gassed, like so many of my people. I should be grateful.'

Out of his depth, Father Ger still blundered duly on.

'I think I know what you mean. Many of our people must have felt stricken after the Famine that laid this country waste. But we did survive. Yet sometimes, surely, you have felt something, a whiff of infinity, a sense of some larger pattern that envelops all poor human accidents into meaning, even the crudity attendant on death?'

'Of God, you mean,' she interjected, curtly enough. 'Oh yes, after making love properly, perhaps, and not only with Knute, but earlier, with Nathan, a young Talmudic student who was killed. For wars create tenderness as well, you know. Do you know the Indian doctrine of *mithuna*, that the act of love can be an insight into the process of creation? Knute can show you those wonderful sculptures from Konarak, executed about the same time as Chartres. Strange how the West celebrated celibacy, the East physical love, both in the name of religion.'

But the priest had buried his head in his hands and she was immediately concerned for him: 'Poor Father Ger, it is not fair to speak of such things to you; the flesh was probably a heresy in your young days. I am very stupid. But there have been other moments.'

'When?' he managed, almost through tears.

'Oh, sailing, when the sea was at force five. In a yacht, however small, one is so conscious of all those tensions, the wind shifting, the waves lurching. The forces of life are so close to one, the danger and the excitement.'

'The forces of life,' he said weakly, 'perhaps we are giving different names to the same thing. God can be both benign and angry, like the sea.'

'And he sends storms, of course, that drown people. One of our most gifted friends was plucked off a rock where he was fishing by a sudden wind. He had already been stricken by polio and didn't swim very well and the sea was high. Maybe he should not have been there, but he was resting from his work and the day was bright. I prefer not to blame anybody: it is the blind structure of life itself, sometimes kind, more often cruel.... My husband may be extreme but he is right; you only begin to make sense of it all when you cease to believe. In sense, in a pattern, in a meaning. Senselessness may be the meaning, the acceptance of the void the beginning of true wisdom. You may call that God if you want to, of course; Nathan spoke of the great Jewish mystic, Isaac the Blind, who saw God in the depths of His nothingness.'

The priest was silent as a stunned bullock. Instead of bringing spiritual aid, he was being instructed by someone much more experienced in the diverse ways of the world, of religion, than himself. How could he answer her, when a part of his spirit was in sympathy with her point of view? But before he tried anything more, she came again to his rescue.

'Father Ger,' she said, affectionately, 'you must not heed too much. I may be feeling bitter. But you came to say goodbye to me, as a good friend. And you feel you have a job to do, in relation to your community, and my extinction. So how can I help you? I'm ready. Then we can say farewell.'

Emaciated, but still full of purpose, Martha Hanger braced herself against her pillows to face the priest. He, in his turn, turned to confront her level, pain-consumed gaze, powerful as an open furnace. And in a few minutes they came to some agreement as to the arrangements of her approaching death, and the ceremonies that could, and could not, be allowed. A bargain was struck between them, down-to-earth as the old-fashioned slapping of palms in the marketplace, Jew and Christian, non-believer and believer, foreigner and native seeking common ground. Knute was not to be insulted; neither was the community that had welcomed them; and Father O'Driscoll was the custodian of that delicate balance. Her last variant made him reel a little, but she had already granted him so much ground that he could only give in, laughing grimly a little at how it might be received. He emerged from the room to where the silent Knute awaited them. Together they finished the bottle of Schnapps.

* * *

From that day forward, the people of Castlehobble came to pay their respects. Knute greeted them briefly but warmly, offering them a glass before they went in to see his wife. The great wooden dining table, the table of his father, and his father's father before him, was laden with Murphy and Guinness, beer of all kinds, large yellow bottles of Paddy and Powers whiskey, a harmless-looking bottle of poteen.

In and out they trooped, consoling, but also, he was surprised to see, especially when they returned from the sickbed, openly smiling. It was as if death were their element, something they could swim in more easily than the vast Atlantic that beat at their doors. They did not get mouldy drunk, they did not overstay their welcome; only Ralph of Ralph's American Bar waxed a little maudlin, remembering his own mother. 'She reminds me of her, you know, Knute, leaving with everything in place, thinking only of those left behind, on this hard earth.

After my mother's death I found little notes everywhere, where she had stored things. And I cried to see them: it was as if she had never left us, and was smiling down from Heaven's Gate.' And he wept, draining another glass.

But he was the exception to a most considerate and orderly procession. As it wound on, day after wearing day, Knute began to wonder about its effects. Was it wearing out Martha, that fount of goodness? No matter how many visitors came, he found her exhausted, but smiling, afterwards. And no one came back: it was a final farewell, which left the bed heaped with flowers, little souvenirs like white heather, four-leafed clover. Peasants though they might be, they were to be congratulated on their courtesy and infinite tact. Deep in some forgotten part of his psyche he felt something stirring, the embers of a religious emotion, which their reverence and respect before the brute fact of death fanned a little. He too bent his head, humbly, before the unknowable, felt briefly the fiercely touching power of simple faith, with its uncomplicated response to the mysterious sorrow we all share. And he thought of Flaubert in his old age looking down at a cradle in the house of his favourite niece and saying sadly: *Ils sont dans le vrai.* The sentimentality of the old, certainly, but perhaps these seemingly simple yokels were right in their way of dealing with death. So he felt for the moment, after they had left and he and his exhausted sleeping wife were alone once more. After he had made the evening meal perhaps he would feel more himself.

* * *

A fortnight later, the day of the funeral dawned, chilly but bright. And now Knute was definitely in poor humour, agitated as a monkey before the many details involved. The last week had been hard, seeing his brave and beloved Martha begin to drift in and out of insensibility. He kept a nightly vigil by her bed, but she no longer knew him, and as he watched the spirit he had loved fade from her eyes, and all the avenues of her wasted body close down, he felt a disconsolate longing for some kind of ceremony, after all.

Although there was always something to keep him occupied, to bring him back to what, normally, he would have called reality. When the doctor confirmed death, there was the ceremony of laying out, and the final funeral arrangements. And now the hearse was standing, dark and shining as a beetle, before the door. And his own old friends had come, the few who lived in Ireland, driving through the early dawn to pay homage to a spirit that they admired, that had influenced their own lives. There were a few embassy officials, for after all, recluse though he might be, Knute Hanger had an international reputation. And some members of the nearest Jewish community, Martha's family being of the older faith.

Discreetly, cars turned and churned before the hall door; instinct and the sight of the gleaming hearse seemed to have brought them out of hiding. On a terrace overlooking the sea, Knute dispensed glasses of dry white wine to his distant guests with a numb but practised politeness that reminded him of his own father. How was he going to get through this of all days? A half of his life had gone, the better half, the dear creature who had endured his bitter moods, now disintegrated into something worse than dust. He could not say if he had loved his wife; he and she had been one, and yet half of that entity was now an extinct and rotting body. Gloomily, he gestured towards the door; after all, he was the master of ceremonies.

Never had he seen his courtyard so full; the bonnets of the cars shone like a shoal of glistening fish. He nodded here and there, recognising Sheila, looking very dignified, Ralph, whom he always had difficulty disassociating from the wooden frame of his bar, the faces of all the people from whom he had bought his goods, the shopkeeper class who seemed to be the backbone of all small Irish towns; a Famine atavism surely?

It did not take long to manage the coffin through the door and then, to his surprise, he was expected to lead in lifting it into the hearse, balanced by other strong, silent men. How absurd all this formality was: there was a corpse, which might just as well be shoved out to sea, or buried in the garden, instead of all this public exploitation of grief, by funeral homes and clergy and so many others! Even work had stopped.

With Martha's coffin safely stowed, under a surprising inundation of flowers, he headed back to the lead black car. In all the teeming mackerel shoal, no one moved, or showed a sign of impatience, waiting with silent understanding for his signal. When he gave it, they began to fall in line, discreetly, deliberately, behind the hearse. As the cortège swung through the narrow streets of Castlehobble, a whole cluster of church bells began to ring out, Protestant and Catholic, ding and dong. If Martha Hanger did not believe in one God, she was being saluted, sent off, by two versions of him.

Along the coast road the cortège sped towards the new graveyard overlooking the sea. Then they climbed out of their cars, stumbling over graves, to where the fresh earth of a newly opened one gaped. Then the ceremony began, in unseasonably bright sunlight.

Usually in Castlehobble all such ceremony was conducted by the priest or parson, both of whom were there. But now Knute stepped forward, speaking rapidly in German. It sounded like poetry, but he paraphrased only a few lines for his audience.

'Today we realise the total absurdity of human existence. One day we are here; tomorrow, gone. We are but butterflies, doomed mayflies dancing on a summer lake. The ultimate proof of the meaninglessness of existence for me is the death of this fine being whom we all admired; she died as bravely as a condemned prisoner. She was an angel but her wings shrivelled in the fire of death. Nothing … absurd.'

He paused but the inhabitants of Castlehobble were already in a state of shock: such language had never been heard in the graveyard. What was Father O'Driscoll doing? He was listening intently to this stream of pagan gibberish. 'From Nietzsche to

Sartre, men have tried to face the harsh facts of nothingness, but I cannot believe. Only a week or so ago I spoke for the last time to Martha: she said how good our life had been. But now it is annihilated, as if she had never lived, we had never loved, and I am angry, angry with this Nobadaddy in the sky.'

Stunned, the folk of Castlehobble saw Knute Hanger shake his fist at the sky. And then another figure stepped forward, not Father Ger, but led by him. It was the cantor of the dwindling Jewish community of Cork, a venerable-looking gentleman with a small skullcap, like the Pope's, only black.

With Father Ger at his side he launched into the noble cadences of the Jewish Office for the Dead, the Kaddish.

He who maketh peace in his high places, may he make peace for us and for all Israel and say ye, Amen.

This time there was no translation. Stiff in the sunlight, the Castlehobble mourners let the waves of language break over them. Some of them had heard at one time or another that Martha was Jewish but they did not really associate it with this strange language, far stranger even to their ears than the German that had marched before it. Were they never to get a look in, be allowed to say a Christian word over an old friend in a Catholic graveyard which sheltered their doubtless outraged own?

At last Father Ger stepped forward. As the gravediggers began to reach for their spades, he started the 'Our Father'. The whole congregation, Catholic and Protestant, joined in, although they noticed that Knute did not. After it was over, he gestured towards the gravediggers again. But Castlehobble was not done yet: one Our Father had not slaked their need to express their grief, to affirm their theological existence. From the depths of the crowd rose the unexpected sound of a prayer in Irish, guttural syllables soon taken up by the waiting throng.

Knute looked up, startled; it was his turn not to understand a word. But for the people of the islands, for whom it was their native tongue, it was still not half enough. They had heard poetry and prayer in every language except the ancient language of the place, the language still heard on the islands that glimmered in the bay, the language of the mountains, the language that had defied English, the language of the faith. If Martha Hanger had chosen to live in Castlehobble and had loved the area above all others in the world, then it would mourn for her in its own way. On that sunny hillside, the ragged keen of the rosary, The Sorrowful Mysteries, swelled to break, slow strophe after strophe, with the heavy stresses of the Gaelic.

* * *

At the post-mortem in Ralph's Bar it was generally agreed that things had gone well, the way they should, the proper way. 'We won,' said the boss, gloatingly; 'that last blast of the Irish, of the old Gaelic, finished them off. It sounded far better than that other old *ráiméis*. What was it, anyway?'

'Hebrew,' said a visitor, sharply. He was an American professor of Jewish ancestry on a sabbatical in Ireland, with a research project on 'Place in Irish Literature'. Castlehobble certainly was a place but it had recently begun to confound him. If it was so welcoming, with refugees from all kinds of different cultures, why this almost simultaneous insistence on the one true faith? He had tagged along to the funeral and found it impressive, the way all the traditions had found their natural place, even atheism. Then why this sudden triumphalism, this small-town piety?

He need not have worried: Martha Hanger had not played her last card. Through the week word got round, as rumour could travel only in Castlehobble, that Father O'Driscoll was going to say something on Sunday about the funeral, preach a sermon about his dear friend Martha's death. Even the late Saturday-night card school, artists, and determined alcoholics, all roused themselves that morning, waiting through, shivering through the length of the Mass for the final statement on Martha's death.

When, after the tinkle of the Mass server's bell had subsided, the priest turned to face his congregation, there was a stir of suspense. For the respectable citizens of Castlehobble, *les bien-pensants* or Holy Marys, still hoped that, despite all evidence to the contrary, the old truth would conquer, converting Martha into an unexpected proof of God's existence, despite that unheard-of behaviour in the graveyard. Maybe there had even been a deathbed conversion? God's ways were often strange, and Father O'Driscoll was as bright as they came, a seminary star who had once won an All-Ireland Medal for the county in Croke Park.

Remembering how often he had slipped past the wiles of players like Mick Mackey and Christy Ring and that this time he was playing for eternal stakes, they would not put it past him to outmanoeuvre a foreigner on the way to his goal.

They were certainly not prepared for what they heard. Row after row of Castlehobble Catholics sat in stiff disbelief as Father Ger warmed to his theme:

'A woman has died amongst us, an extraordinary woman. A woman whom we all loved, generous, charitable, and as she proved at the end, brave. There was a difference between us. She sincerely believed, like her husband, that God did not exist. You may think that this is because they lived in the great world, and saw things that we are spared in our green isle.'

Was Father Ger going to turn his argument around, to show how blessed we were in our geographical isolation; had Saint Patrick not said that Ireland would be drowned, not burned at the end of the world? But no — he continued, with fire and fervour, to defend Martha Hanger for not believing in God.

'A great English poet and laureate declared "There lives more faith in honest doubt,/ Believe me, than in half the creeds": that was the convinced position of Martha Hanger and her husband.' Whatever bargain had been struck in that sickroom, Father Ger kept to it with a vengeance; as well as a swingeing defence of atheism, he used Martha's example to lash his incredulous flock.

'You may think they disbelieved because they had seen the cruelty of man in far places. But our own brand of small-scale evil exists here, the butcher who slaughters the trembling lamb without thinking, the merchant who systematically overcharges, the factory farmer who despoils the fields, the drunkards on the farmer's dole, the ruthless property developer, the brutal school-master, our association of unreformed alcoholics, who sometimes beat their wives and children when they are hauled home; the list is endless. And I have not included the mistreatment of animals for sport, for which this country is famous; remember the great lines of another English poet and, dare I say it again, saint? What would Blake have thought of coursing? "Each outcry of the hunted Hare / A fibre from the brain does tear."

'So don't think for a moment that any victory was gained at this good woman's funeral. The ills that the Hangers have fought against all their lives are present in miniature in this village, painted over with piety. And it is that lesson we must learn from her death, endured so humbly. I say to all of you that if you were as sincere in your beliefs, as brave in your end as Martha Hanger, then Castlehobble would indeed be a wonder-ful place. Her presence is still amongst us because she is as near as I have seen to —'

He paused while his dumbfounded flock waited for those final words which would ring in their minds for years.

'Martha Hanger, in her simplicity and dedication, to her family and to others, was as near as I have seen to what you call a saint. She was selfless, free from our corrosive malice, a giving spirit. She had that charity of which Saint Paul speaks: today she stands in the presence of God — or his absence, as she would have seen it. May we all strive to do as well in this world. I know that I will always try to follow her example.'

With tears in his eyes, but pride in his voice, Father Gerard O'Driscoll turned his back to the altar. The church was silent.

Also Published by
Wolfhound Press

Death of a Chieftain
& Other Stories

These nine stories extend from Northern Ireland to Dublin, and even, in the daring title story, to Mexico. They focus on such compelling and diverse themes as the conspiracy of sadism between schoolmaster and schoolchildren; the fantasy world of a lonely farm boy; political scheming in a city office; the struggles of a gifted artist in bohemian Dublin. 'The Cry', an astonishingly prescient story, is one of the first to describe the beginnings of the Troubles, and 'An Occasion of Sin', written in the voice of a young French woman confronting Irish attitudes to sex, is a small masterpiece. But it is the title story which dazzles most of all. Anticipating magic realism, this tour de force describes the astonishing Bernard Corunna Coote and his Mexican campaign to establish that the Irish founded America!

Two of the stories in this collection have been filmed: 'A Change of Management' by RTÉ, and 'The Cry' by the BBC.

John Montague's *Death of a Chieftain & Other Stories* is undoubtedly one of the most important collections of short stories to emerge from an Irish writer in the twentieth century.

'A landmark for the future.'
The Irish Times

ISBN: 0-86327-673-3

Available from
Wolfhound Press
68 Mountjoy Square
Dublin 1
Tel: +353 1 874 0354; Fax: + 353 1 872 0207